W9-AXS-519

"See reason here. Murray's my agent. I can't just disappear. What am I supposed to tell him if he calls me back?"

"Do you really want me to answer that?" Rook's insanely desirable face was a study in pure menace.

"Well, I have to tell him something." Viva blew at a curl that bounced between her brows. "He practically has to beg me to take breaks. He'd never believe I just ran off and—"

"Not even if you told him you ran off with me?"

Openmouthed, Viva could only stare.

Rook took advantage of the quiet. "Tell him we're rekindling the flame. Tell him…tell him I threatened to tie you to my bed until you agreed to go along and you believed me. I think that's a threat I've followed through on a time or two, isn't it?"

Viva tried to speak, laugh, something…but she failed at every attempt. She ran her tongue over her lips and tried speaking again. "He'd know that's not true. He'd know I'm lying—"

Any further argument was silenced once he kissed her and her tongue was otherwise engaged with his. Rook had taken command of her wrist and tugged her across the brief space separating them on the desk. Seamless and confident, he settled her across the broad width of his thigh, making her straddle the limb in a ruthless, brazen manner.

Dear Reader,

I'd like to start this letter off with a big THANK YOU! Your embrace of the Provocative Series has meant so very much. *Provocative Attraction* and the stories preceding it—*Provocative Territory* and *Provocative Passion*—really hit me out of nowhere and took me along for a ride crafted heavily by the characters.

The journey continues with Rook and Viva's story. Questions are answered amid the heavy tension and regrets experienced by our hero and heroine. Viva Hail has got a lot on her plate. There's the new season of her hit show to prepare for, turmoil and mistrust brewing between her and her agent, and then there's Rook Lourdess—the man she loves…the man she left.

It's always such a treat returning to the worlds I've created. This return was definitely a treat—one that I hope you'll fully enjoy.

Let me know what you think!

Love,

AlTonya

altonya@lovealtonya.com

Provocative
ATTRACTION

AlTonya Washington

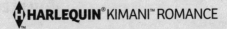
HARLEQUIN® KIMANI™ ROMANCE

If you purchased this book without a cover you should be aware that this book is stolen property. It was reported as "unsold and destroyed" to the publisher, and neither the author nor the publisher has received any payment for this "stripped book."

Recycling programs
for this product may
not exist in your area.

ISBN-13: 978-0-373-86451-5

Provocative Attraction

Copyright © 2016 by AlTonya Washington

All rights reserved. The reproduction, transmission or utilization of this work in whole or in part in any form by any electronic, mechanical or other means, now known or hereinafter invented, including xerography, photocopying and recording, or in any information storage or retrieval system, is forbidden without written permission. For permission please contact Harlequin Kimani, 225 Duncan Mill Road, Toronto, Ontario M3B 3K9, Canada.

This is a work of fiction. Names, characters, places and incidents are either the product of the author's imagination or are used fictitiously, and any resemblance to actual persons, living or dead, business establishments, events or locales is entirely coincidental.

® and TM are trademarks of Harlequin Enterprises Limited or its corporate affiliates. Trademarks indicated with ® are registered in the United States Patent and Trademark Office, the Canadian Intellectual Property Office and in other countries.

For questions and comments about the quality of this book please contact us at CustomerService@Harlequin.com.

HARLEQUIN®
www.Harlequin.com

Printed in U.S.A.

AlTonya Washington has been a romance novelist for over eleven years. She's been nominated for numerous awards and has won two RT Reviewers' Choice Awards for her novels *Finding Love Again* and *His Texas Touch*. AlTonya lives in North Carolina and works as a college reference librarian. This author wears many hats, but being a mom is her favorite job.

Books by AlTonya Washington

Harlequin Kimani Romance

Visit the Author Profile page at Harlequin.com for more titles.

Prologue

Philadelphia, PA

"She's not doing commercials because she's interested in keeping the public informed on what's new at the market, Rook."

Rook Lourdess flexed his fingers once, twice. It was a habit he'd learned had the remarkable tendency to alleviate the need to clench a fist and follow through with connecting said fist to the jaw belonging to the unfortunate soul who'd riled him. Lately, that had been Murray Dean—former friend, former partner and present traitor.

"What are you getting out of this?" Rook asked once the need to punch Murray had passed.

Murray gave a half shrug. "Not a damn thing—"

"Not yet."

Murray's jaw muscles clenched noticeably then. "I'm not blind, Rook, and neither is Viva. She's got a chance in there." He jabbed a thumb over his shoulder toward a long corridor that opened into an expansive main room to the party where most of the guests still mingled.

"You tell me, what were the odds of coming along to one of your boring-ass client events and running into one of the biggest movie producers in the country?" Murray continued.

Rook felt his jaw flex He had no handy remedy to ease the action that reflex usually prefaced. "Did she need you to tell me that?" he queried, his voice low and mildly lethal.

Murray grinned. "She doesn't know I'm out here, but since her getting your attention at a client event is even less likely than her getting it when you're supposed to be *off* the job..." Again, he shrugged. "I thought it'd help to step up."

"Help her? Or help you?"

Murray snorted a laugh through his nostrils. "Me? What am I supposed to get out of it?"

"I don't know." Rook's gaze narrowed, reflecting a jolting amber glint. "It's something, though. You do nothing without a reason."

Bristling at the barb, Murray raised a brow. "Are we getting around to my leaving the security firm, now?"

"Leaving, huh?" Rook rolled a broad shoulder in a casual shrug. "A leave that was followed by your very generous offer to the rest of the guys to come on over to your neck of the woods."

Agitation more noticeable then, Murray rubbed at a clean-shaved albeit weak jaw. "And they threw my offer back in my face," he admitted. At that point, it was useless to deny the unethical moves he'd orchestrated. "What's the problem now, Rook? None of them were willing to jump ship. You're lucky to have a group of very loyal men."

"Yeah, they've all been loyal. All but one. The one I never thought would stab me in the back."

"Because I wanted something for myself?" Murray sounded incredulous.

"No. Because you wanted what belonged to me." Viva Hail, his girlfriend of four years, was an aspiring actress.

"Ahh…and no one takes or even looks at what belongs to Rook Lourdess without paying the stiffest penalties. Guess I should watch my back now after standing up to you about Viva.

"Do you know how on edge she's been about talking to you about Fritz Vossler's production company?" Murray went on when Rook remained silent. "She thought you'd be pissed. Guess she was right."

"To know that, you must've been watching her pretty close." Rook flexed his fingers again, but the fist clenched anyway.

Murray's shrug regained its casual resonance. "Didn't take much watching to know that. Her eyes went back and forth between you and Vossler a good five minutes in there. When you headed off to see to more business, you could all but see how relieved she was."

"Murray."

Both Rook and Murray turned at the sound of the soft but husky feminine voice that had called out.

Viva Hail stood in the foyer where Murray had cornered Rook after Rook's brief chat with his client and security team on hand for the evening's gala event. Rook's client represented a well-known Philadelphia charity that had national appeal to those with ties to the theater and film industries.

Viva shook her head once in Murray's direction.

Murray turned back to Rook. "Listen, man," he began in a tone far more humble than the one he'd used previously. "In spite of everything, I do care about you guys. I was just trying to help." He left Rook with a quick smile, headed to Viva and brushed her arm when he drew near. "I'll be at the bar," he told her.

"I hear you need my attention, is that right?" Rook considered Murray's departing form before looking back to Viva. "I'm only working off his insight, but he seems to have a crap load of it." He made an effort to come down off some of his frustration. "Be straight with me, V. Have I done something to make you afraid to talk to me?"

"No. No, Rook. Please don't think that."

"Then tell me what to think." He threw another look toward the corridor. "When the hell did you and Murray get so close?"

"Since he became the manager of Fritz Vossler's East Coast security division."

Rook ignored the tightening of his jaw muscle then. Word had reached him of Murray snagging the big fish a few weeks back. "What's that got to do with you?"

Viva began a slow walk around the perimeter of the townhome's foyer. The hem of her empire-waist crimson gown swished elegantly about her curvy frame as she moved. "Mr. Vossler and his people are scouting for fresh talent, and anyone they sign is privy to all the perks his West Coast assets receive. Security is one of them."

"Again, what's that got to do with you, V?" His manner proved to her he already had the answer.

"Vossler just asked me to sign with his company."

"Just asked?"

She smiled, understanding. "He asked weeks ago."

Rook smiled then too and commenced his own slow pace of the foyer. "Weeks ago…guess that's what he was talking to you about the other night at Jazzy B's."

Viva inhaled sharper than she realized. Sometimes she forgot how scarily perceptive her boyfriend was. "He goes there a lot when he's in town."

"Right. Looking for new talent and all."

"Rook… Don't make this harder."

"'This.'" Rook stopped his pacing. "Exactly what is 'this,' V? Telling me you signed with a producer? I don't think Murray would've been looking as smug as he was if it was only about that."

Viva watched him, amazed and wondering how he read a person so easily. Resolved, she gathered what remained of her struggling courage and decided to get it over with. "Mr. Vossler offered me a part—not a commercial but a *real* part. Shooting starts in two weeks on location…in Rio."

Rook felt the blow her words dealt him. He forced himself to recover quickly. "Brazil. Congrats."

"Rook—"

"How long will you be gone?"

"Five months," she said after a split second of hesitation. "We head out to Los Angeles right after that to finish filming and postproduction. That'll take another month or so."

Rook resumed his stroll. Then his steps took him in a wide circle around Viva. "That's a lot of prepping to do in two weeks. Shots, passport, your job."

She smiled again. There was no humor in the gesture. She knew what he was getting at. "I've done all that already," she said.

"And at no time was there an opportunity to tell me?"

"I didn't know how—" She bristled anew when he erupted into cold laughter.

"Didn't know how? Hell, V, I guess we've got more problems than I thought."

"I don't want this to ruin us."

The small, bewildered tone of her voice squeezed his heart. "How could you think it wouldn't, babe? Our communication is already in the crapper. You being out of the country for half the year isn't gonna help that."

"I have to take this, Rook. It's what I've been working for."

"Right. After all, you're not just doing commercials because you're interested in keeping the public informed on what's new at the market." At her confused look, he grimaced and shook his head. "So I'm losing you to this?"

"I don't want that." Viva clasped her hands between her breasts and moved to him. "It could work."

"We barely see each other as it is. I'm busy all the damn time getting the firm on point and that's done no favors to our relationship." He paused to smooth a hand across his hair, a mass of soft, close-cropped twists capping his head. "Only thing that's kept us together, V, is you having a less demanding job. That's over now."

Viva felt something chill inside her at his use of the word *over*. Again, she grabbed hold of fledgling courage. "What are you saying? If I take the job, we're done?" she asked.

"Don't put that on me, V. You know how shaky things are between us right now. You know as well as I do that we won't survive another blow. But you can forget about me letting you go. I'm afraid that's a decision that'll be made for us. My actions have already set the path. I guess yours will put us on it."

Her vision was a blur then. He was right. They'd been passing ships for months. Her going to work for Jazmina Beaumont's gentlemen's club had certainly not been the best decision. The fact that he'd become increasingly busy building his firm had taken his mind off the concerns he had with her waitressing there.

They wouldn't survive this, but he was saying that he refused to be the one to put that nail into their coffin. Could she?

"When are you due to leave?"

She barely heard his voice cut through the storm of her thoughts. "End of the week," she said.

Rook had pretty much schooled his expression but the devastation in his entrancing amber stare was unmistakable.

Viva knew she had the answer to her question then. She *could* put that nail in their coffin. She already had.

Chapter 1

Philadelphia, PA
Six years later

Rook Lourdess knew his rich laughter had the tendency to carry whether he was in the midst of absolute silence or chaos. Both environments proved to be appropriate descriptors that night. His laughter carried out from the party still going strong indoors to the terrace that somehow maintained its serene quiet.

"Sounds good," he was saying to whomever he spoke to through the mobile he held to his ear. "Sure you don't need me there?" Rook nodded, listening to the caller's response.

"I guess that'll work, seeing as how I've got that five a.m. conference call…Italy," he added, following a few more seconds of silence.

"Yeah, they sound serious. I keep waiting on them to call and tell me they made a mistake…Ha! I appreciate that," he said once more silence had passed from his end.

"Forget it!" Rook's laughter clung to the words. "I don't care how much you lay on the flattery, you're not goin'…Nah, B, I need you to stay here and hold it all down at the firm, but don't worry, we'll be having that talk soon enough…Yeah…" A somber element crept into Rook's voice then. "Yeah, I'm not looking forward to it either. Listen, man, I better get goin'. Just be ready with that report by tomorrow afternoon. I want to get this all put to bed before I leave… All right, talk to you then." Following another brief stint of silence and more laughter, Rook was easing the phone into a back trouser pocket. He didn't head back to the party, but stood on the terrace and looked out into the night. Moving closer to the stone railing, he inhaled deeply and smiled.

Robust cheer sounded indoors, but Rook resisted the tug of the partygoers and reminded himself that he needed to hit the sack.

His Italian contacts would be speaking with him at 11:00 a.m. their time. He had to be sharp as possible by 5:00 a.m. That wouldn't happen unless he headed for his car and home right then.

Rook was turning to make his exit down the terrace's wide steps when he heard her.

"Italy, huh?"

So much for getting to sleep anytime soon, Rook thought when he saw Viva Hail seated and looking coolly lovely from her spot on one of the cushioned chaises dotting the terrace.

Seeing her never failed to seriously screw with his sleep. Whether it was on the big screen or small didn't matter. Seeing her in person...well, he shuddered to think of what his Italian business associates would think of him when they spoke in eight hours. He wouldn't be getting that full night of sleep he'd hoped for.

"V." His voice was soft, unlike the sound of the blood rushing in his ears.

"Sorry for eavesdropping." Viva lifted a manicured hand a few centimeters from her lap and let it fall back to the beige silk pants she wore. "I was out here when you came to the terrace. I didn't mean to listen in."

"It wasn't anything top secret." He moved closer to where she sat.

"Was it business or pleasure?" Viva didn't close her eyes in mortification when she heard the question trip off her tongue, but mortification rolled in hot and heavy waves all the same. Pleasure was always a given when it involved Rook Lourdess. She knew that well enough, didn't she? Again, she waved. "Sorry to pry."

Rook grinned. "You're not."

"So, um, what part of Italy are you visiting?"

"Belluno."

"Ah..." Viva smiled and closed her eyes as she nodded. "That's not far from Cortina. It's really beautiful this time of year."

"So I hear." Hands hidden in the deep pockets of his dark trousers, Rook strolled closer. "Has your work taken you there?" He somehow resisted asking if her knowledge of the place was on a personal level.

Viva was already nodding. "I did a movie there two

years ago while the show was on hiatus. An ensemble-cast thing. It was fun."

"Ensemble cast, like the show. How's that going?"

"Very well. We've been a truly blessed bunch."

"So no talk of finales anytime soon?"

"If only." Viva threw back her head and sighed. "I was sure we'd be done after season four with everyone so busy with other successful projects, but…" She flexed her fingers over the pants that matched a shimmering blazer. "The audience still loves us, the ratings are dynamite… I'd say we'll be a bunch of kick-ass secret agents well into our nineties."

Laughter hummed around the terrace then.

"So, um, are you visiting Italy on new business for the firm?" Viva figured additional prying couldn't hurt at that point.

"Remains to be seen," was all he could share before the party volume grew to a maddening pitch and tipped over to deafening.

Rook and Viva realized the French doors had opened as chief of detectives Sophia Hail exited with congratulatory cheers behind her.

"There she is!" Rook's voice carried across the terrace as he closed the distance to Sophia and enveloped her in a bear hug. "The news is in the air. Congratulations. It's a good night for the Philly PD," he said and kissed her cheek.

Sophia, the recent recipient of an unexpected promotion to chief of detectives, wore a grin that seemed to make her entire face glow.

"Thanks." Sophia laughed, returning Rook's tight squeeze. "But I can't let any of these accolades go to my head, no matter how good they feel floating up there."

The accolades were well deserved. Sophia and her team had just come leagues closer to wrapping up a complex money-laundering scheme that had implicated several members of the force. Sophia's predecessor was among them.

Viva stepped up to draw her younger sister into a tight squeeze. "Congratulations, sweetie. Are you done for the night?" she asked once they broke from the embrace.

"Hardly," Sophia sighed in a manner that sang with satisfaction. "I just wanted to get back. Mama went to all this trouble to put together this party for me. My people can handle the wrap-up and I'll be back at the job in the morning."

Sophia slid Rook another smile and squeezed his arm. "Think you can fit me in for a quick talk sometime tomorrow?"

"Sure. Might be early. I've got a five a.m. chat to Europe tomorrow."

Sophia whistled, her eyes twinkling. "Good luck with that."

"I'll need it." Rook smoothed a hand over his chest as though the idea pained him. "I should've been in bed hours ago."

"Well, I plan to make it an early day myself," Sophia said. "I'll make time whenever you can drop in."

"Count on it." He nodded before gracing Viva's face with his arresting gaze.

Sophia appeared as though she could read the look. "So, V, I'll just see you inside, okay?"

"No, you stay," Rook said. "I'm the one who needs

to get going." He gave Viva a smile. "Good seeing you. How long before you leave?"

Viva lifted her shoulders and let the move hold a few seconds before she lowered them.

"I'm not sure yet."

"Don't leave without saying goodbye, okay?"

"Count on it," she returned the earlier confirmation he'd given to her sister. With effort, she kept a cool smile in place while he said good-night to Sophia and made his way from the terrace.

"He hasn't changed."

Sophia smiled at Viva's remark. "Did you think he would?" she asked.

The ebony flecks in Viva's warm chocolate stare appeared to sparkle beneath a sudden nudge of emotion. "I prayed he wouldn't after everything that happened. Sophia, um…is he, um…is he seeing anybody?"

Sophia looked off in the direction where Rook had taken his exit. "I'd have to ask Tigo," she said, referring to her fiancé and one of Rook's oldest friends, Santigo Rodriguez. "Far as I know there hasn't been anyone since you."

Viva shot her sister a stunned expression.

"No one *steady* since you," Sophia qualified.

Viva wasn't wholly convinced of that either, but such a statement was easier to swallow than one suggesting there had been *no one* since her.

Rook Lourdess was a presence. He exuded a power that went beyond the obvious potency presented by the striking breadth of his physique. His massive build, combined with a jolting stare and remarkably crafted face, had a talent for unsettling women as thoroughly as it mesmerized them.

Still, it was the subtle aspect of his persona, Viva believed, that was even more alluring. Unarguably, the face and body were difficult acts to follow. The body was a well-honed six and a half feet of solid muscle sheathed in a rich caramel-toned casing that was only rivaled by the face. It was surrounded by a halo of blue-black that, despite the efforts to keep it close-cropped, remained an unruly cap of waves.

The carefully crafted face was accentuated by a heavy-lidded amber stare of such a hue, it seemed almost translucent. The nose emphasized strong, high cheekbones offset by a generous and fully kissable mouth—one Viva remembered was capable of exerting the most extreme forms of pleasure and release.

She cleared her throat, not sure if the moan she'd just given in to had been overheard by her sister or merely an echo in her own head.

"Sure you don't want to catch up to him? He probably hasn't gotten to his car yet."

Viva snorted. "If I punch you, would that be considered assaulting an officer?"

Sophia gave in to a sly grin. "I'd make the charges stick."

Viva countered with a shrug. "I'm sure I could find a lawyer to get me off."

"Mmm… I thought you'd want Rook for that."

A few seconds of silence followed the playfully lurid comment. Then, the sisters gave in to wild laughter that was as much about amusement as it was about happiness over the fact that they were together and that so many troubling aspects of the past were finally being laid to rest. So many…but not all.

"So did I interrupt anything here?" Sophia clasped her hands and eyed the terrace speculatively. "Anything…promising?"

Again, Viva snorted. "If you count small talk promising."

"Ah, honey." Sophia moved close to drop an arm around Viva's shoulders and squeezed. "I'm sorry."

"No need. It's for the best."

"I don't think you believe that." Sophia used her height advantage to drop a kiss to the top of her sister's head. "Are you saying you hold absolutely *no* hope that you guys could have what you once did?"

"It's been a long time."

"And? A lot of time passed between me and Tigo too."

Viva conceded with a smile. "Fair enough, but it still wouldn't be a good idea, Soapy."

"Not a good idea?" Sophia challenged once she'd chuckled over the name Viva had given her before she could correctly pronounce her little sister's name. "You *did* just see the man, right? I'm surprised he walked out of here alone with all the…attention I saw him getting before I had to hustle out of here earlier."

Viva moved to the terrace railing and looked out into the night as though she were seeing Rook there. "There're things I don't want him to know. Ever. Things that might hurt him and that'll make me feel like more of an ass for leaving than I already do."

Intrigued, Sophia's gray eyes narrowed, all teasing elements leaving her face. "Any details you can share?" She joined Viva at the railing. "Is this about Murray?"

"This all happened near the beginning of my career." She slid her sister a sly smile. "I promise there aren't any moves I wish I didn't make. At least none of the truly graphic variety. There are choices I made, though, and later wished I hadn't. Choices I may not have made if working for Jazzy B's hadn't made me immune to certain signs."

"And that's Mom and Dad talking now."

"Maybe," Viva bumped her side to Sophia's. "Parents can make a lot of sense sometimes."

Sophia folded her arms over her chest and turned to lean back against the rail. "So are you going to let these old choices keep you from going back to the man you love?"

"Soap, it's been six—"

"Back to the man who still loves you?" Sophia interrupted. "V, these *things* you mentioned… Murray was with you at the beginning. Are you sure that doesn't have anything to do with this present mess?"

Viva was shaking her head. "This particular choice doesn't have much to do with Murray but some of my other choices… If I hadn't made them, you probably wouldn't have what you need to put your case to bed."

"Hold it, V." Sophia took her sister's shoulders and gave her a slight shake. "I can damn well put my case to bed without drawing you into it."

"Maybe I want to be drawn in." Unshakeable determination sharpened Viva's star-quality features. "I only knew Murray a little through Rook before we started working together at my first production company. It didn't take long for me to see that he could be a shark, but that's a commodity in my world and I didn't shy away from him because I wanted my career and I correctly guessed that he could give me one."

"Hey." Sophia gave Viva another tug. "You're the only one responsible for your career."

"Thanks, Soap, but Murray really is very good at what he does. He made a very successful move from security to talent representation. Over the years, I've come to consider him as a very good friend as well as my agent."

"And that may make it harder for you to believe he could be involved in all the rest," Sophia warned.

"Why'd he do it, Sophia?" Viva tugged her fingers through the light brown coils framing her face. "Why'd he risk doing something that could take away his freedom?"

"Some folks can't resist the sparkle, no matter how much they have. A little more is always a good thing."

"Yeah." Viva thought of how that point had pertained to her when she'd started getting noticed—when the sparkle of real celebrity began to twinkle her way. It should've been enough, but Sophia was right. More always seemed better. She supposed it was the same for Murray. Too bad his quest for more sparkle had turned him into a criminal.

"I have to be part of this, Sophia."

"All right." Sophia nodded. "But if that's the case, I'm going to need you to agree to any and all requests I make pertaining to your own well-being."

Viva bit her lip before acquiescing with a hesitant nod.

"I mean it, V. Take it or leave it."

"Okay…but only on the condition that you don't let any of this newfound power over me go to your head."

"I'll try." To Viva's ears the words held little promise. "But give me any of that A-list actress diva attitude and I'll put you on house arrest."

"Such a hard-ass," Viva accused.

"I'm worse." Sophia waved off the insult. "I'm a bride. I'm about to start getting very anal about things being perfect. Keeping my maid of honor alive goes at the top of that list."

Viva gave herself over to laughter. The gesture was soon being echoed by Sophia and the sisters tucked into another hug.

Rook gave a quick prayer of thanks when he pulled the Suburban into the parking spot outside his condo. The need for sleep had latched on harder and heavier the second his butt had hit the driver's seat.

It was a blessing that he hadn't hit anything or been pulled over for a suspected DUI considering how wiped he was. He'd been looking forward to an exceptional night of sleep, but he now feared that would be a fruitless endeavor. Finding Viva Hail on that terrace had hit him like a brick to his gut.

He'd known she was in town. He'd run into her while his team had supplied security for her sister. Not until that night had the true force of her being back really hit him. She'd always been able to read him so well and he wondered if she could see how out of it he was earlier.

Resting back on the seat, Rook reminisced on how her perception intrigued as well as annoyed him. He wasn't a man who enjoyed having others get inside his head.

Viva Hail wasn't just any *other*. No, she wasn't just any other and how had he honored that so long ago? By giving her an ultimatum. No…it hadn't been a blatant "take it or leave it" ultimatum, but he'd damn well known what he was doing when he gave her that bull about the decision being made for them and that *her* actions would put them on the path his had already set.

He'd let her think the rest was all her decision and whatever the final outcome, it was on her. The simple truth was he just didn't want to see her reaction when he owned up to her dead-on perception that he really was set on them being done if she left. How was he supposed to tell her a thing like that?

Furthermore, how were they supposed to make a relationship work if she'd gone along? Every day she'd regret the choice—the sacrifice—she'd made for their relationship.

Groaning, Rook left the SUV and faintly celebrated the fact that his eyes were still weighted by sleep. He made it to the quiet, understated elegance of the lobby. His condominium complex was an impressive layout of four separate skyscrapers interconnected by a series of moving walkways all joining at the lobby. The walkways were basically for aesthetic purposes—the lobby also housed an elevator bay to accommodate those who opted out of taking the scenic route to their respective towers.

Rook selected an elevator, smiling as the warmth and familiarity of home settled into his bones. Work kept him from arriving during the evening rush; his day job wasn't a normal nine to five after all. He didn't mind as the schedule usually allowed him to arrive once things had settled down.

The place had a way of enveloping him in a solitude he'd felt in few other places that he'd lived. Perhaps that was because it was the place he and Viva had settled in when they'd moved in together all those years ago.

Plush, yet functional carpeting offset by the warm, golden lighting, glowed from mahogany-based sconces against mocha-painted walls. The allure of the place had been Viva's doing. Her presence had lent it the truest sense of warmth and home. Only to himself could he admit he'd do anything to feel that again. His current residence, void of her, was a poor substitute, but better than nothing.

The elevator dinged and sent him on a nonstop ascent to his floor which held only one additional unit aside from his own. He and Viva had happily worked like dogs to maintain the utilities and other incidental expenses associated with such a place. As they'd both come from affluent families, snagging digs at one of the most enviable addresses in the city had raised few brows.

Rook's parents, Kendall and Elise Lourdess, had handled payments on the property. They had fallen as in love with Viva as her parents, Gerald and Veronica Hail, had fallen for Rook.

There was little comment made about them living together unmarried. Assumptions ran high on both sides that nuptials would be forthcoming. Then Viva went to waitress for Jazzy B's Gentlemen's Club and had caught the eye of several men. One introduced her to the camera. Offers for commercials began to flood and their relationship, as Rook saw it, began a slow and terrible transformation that had signaled its end.

Chapter 2

"Guess I work better on low fuel."

Burt Larkin chuckled over his boss's insight. "I'll take that to mean the call went well."

"Guess so." Rook held the phone away as he yawned. "We spent the last twenty minutes of the call discussing my trip over there."

"Have I told you how lucky you are?"

Rook laughed. "Only about a million times."

"So will you grace us with your presence today? It's not every day me and the guys see someone as lucky as you."

"How long am I gonna have to put up with these jokes?" Rook said following another few moments of robust laughter.

"Please," Burt sighed. "We haven't even started yet."

Rook countered with a playful groan. "Well, I'll

be in as soon as I leave the cop shop," he told his second in command.

Burt reciprocated the groan. "Should we have bail money handy just in case?"

"Hmph, not this time. I'm only goin' in for a quick talk with the new chief of Ds."

"Ah…this about what went down last night?"

"Not sure. Sophia was kind of vague when she asked for the meeting, but that's probably because Viva was standing right there."

"Well, well." Surprise registered in Burt's twangy voice. "What was that like?"

"I'll give you a hint—it's why I didn't sleep worth a damn last night."

"Right." Burt let the conversation end there, no doubt knowing how touchy the subject was for his boss. "So…at this point, our report is complete and we'll await your input."

"I think from here on out the chief's got her security well in hand. I'll review and sign the report when I get there."

Lourdess Securities, known as L Sec by the clients it handled in the private, public and entertainment sectors, had been hired to provide its coveted brand of protection to Sophia Hail following her recent promotion. The detective's investigation into an ever-increasingly sensational money-laundering scheme had taken root. Threats had also taken root to encourage the insightful detective to back off her inquiries. As a result, Philadelphia DA Paula Starker had sought out Rook and his team to shadow her colleague and friend.

"The rest of the team is in agreement that Chief Hail's normal security detail will be enough, but we're good with maintaining our posts until a certain person of interest is apprehended."

Rook knew what Burt was saying. The team had been on hand the previous evening when several arrests were made in the case. The team knew that Sophia's investigation had led her to Murray Dean.

"According to what I heard last night, our old friend Dean has a role to play in all this." Burt told him.

"Yeah…" Rook's tone was light, but his agreement on Murray's involvement was firm.

"Will this be a new problem for you and Viva, man?"

Rook laughed. "We've had no problems for at least six years, B," he reminded his friend and business associate.

"True, and it'd be a shame to have new upsets weighing in when you're about to pull up stakes for Italy."

"Yeah…" Rook voiced his light agreement once more, but offered no further opinion.

"So I'll see you later?" Burt seemed to take the cue that his boss was all chatted out.

"Yeah, B, thanks." Rook added a goodbye and ended the call.

Setting aside his mobile, he rubbed tired eyes and yawned for what had to be the fiftieth time since he'd awakened that morning. Smirking, he turned the word over in his head… *Awakened.* More like arisen from a troubled bout with his bedsheets.

Dreams had been shoved aside for a night of tossing, turning and images of Viva Hail attacking his subconscious. The sleep he'd hoped to indulge in had flitted away without so much as a toodle-loo when he'd strolled through the quiet, broad space of the condo to the bedroom.

The bed conjured the first of many images—Viva sprawled out on her stomach and sleeping him off after an enthusiastic session of sex, covers twisted with erotic intricacy about her shapely calves and lush thighs. Sleep for him then had become a wish with no possibility of materializing.

Her face and body were irrevocably stamped on his brain. They would never be removed and he wouldn't want them to be. Such a thing was assured when he'd seen her a few weeks earlier rushing into her sister's place. She'd been staying with Sophia while visiting Philadelphia. The image of her had then been reasserted last night. He recalled seeing her on the terrace, knowing how close he was to reaching out to take her to him before they were interrupted.

The body, still curvy and lush, was even more alluring. The added muscle tone was attributed to her active career and the physical demands of the roles she secured. The face was a work of natural glamour enhanced by coils of light brown curls surrounding a honey-toned face.

It was a face that needed no man-made accents. The mouth was a study in erotic art as were the high cheekbones and small nose that upturned just a fraction at the tip. Big brown eyes were offset by ebony flecks that sparkled amid upset or…arousal.

No, getting to sleep last night was an idiot's assumption. And what of Italy? Another assumption? The trip was about more than adding a boost to his business. L Sec was a bona fide success. The investment his parents had made in the dream of their only child had been a smart move. The elder Lourdesses had earned back their seed money many times over.

Rook knew the truth and he suspected most of his executive team knew it, as well. He was running. Two of his best friends had found women with whom they wanted to spend the rest of their lives. It had become too much to remain in the place where he'd lost the woman with whom he wanted to spend the rest of his. The memories that had sustained him for the last six years had at last become a series of ropes knotted into a noose of increasing tightness.

Yes, he was running. Italy was far enough to ease the memories, even if the distance wouldn't totally remove them. Italy, for him, signified freedom. Freedom from a past he was desperate to exorcise.

Of course, all that was before he'd seen Viva again. Rook glimpsed his hand and realized he'd clenched a fist without feeling the move take hold. His temper was elevating to boiling point. It was another of those ropes that were starting to develop choking intensity.

He was considering some time in the gym to trample the blackness clouding his mind, when his phone chimed, reminding him of the meeting with Sophia.

Once more Rook studied his hand. Flexing it slightly, he cast a lingering look toward the door at the end of the hall that led to his home gym. Pivoting then, Rook headed away from the door as though he were being hunted.

* * *

"Are you sure I can't bring you anything, Mr. Lourdess? We've got soft drinks and an array of bottled waters if you prefer that to the chief's coffee."

"I'm good, but thank you." Rook's smile exhibited genuine appreciation when he addressed the attractive brunette from his seat before the wide walnut desk.

"Well, you be sure to let me know if you change your mind."

When the woman left, Rook graced the chief with a look of earnest ease that lent credence to the fact that he had no interest in the magnitude of his appeal.

Sophia's grin was equally earnest as she observed him. "I should apologize for my assistant. She's not always so obvious in her appraisal of my guests."

Rook tossed up a hand, another clear indicator that he thought nothing of the assistant's overt flirting. "It's good to have a talent for making the guests feel special."

"Mmm…" Sophia sipped at her coffee, nodding. "To be on the safe side, I think I'll tell her your heart belongs to my sister."

"Sophia," Rook groaned, leaning back his head a fraction. "Tell me this isn't why you wanted to see me."

"No, not exactly." Sophia studied the steaming liquid in her ceramic mug. "But anyone who saw you guys last night would know there's still love there."

"Does it matter?" Rook asked after a moment's consideration.

Sophia reared back in the scooping burgundy suede chair set behind a desk of impressive breadth befitting the new chief of detectives. "The way you feel about my sister could matter quite a bit in light of what I'm about to ask you."

"Which is?" Shifting a bit in the boxy chair, same color and finish as the one Sophia occupied, Rook felt equal parts expectant and hesitant.

Sophia left her chair to round the desk and ease her hip down to one corner. "V didn't come to town just visiting. She wants to make a statement and testify if need be against Murray Dean."

"What the hell, Sophia?" Rook's voice was a ragged whisper. His arresting gaze was hard and fixed on Sophia then.

"While she's worked with Murray, she's witnessed some things. Things that could tie him up nice and snug to some of Philadelphia's finest who're tangled in this laundering case."

Rook left his chair. Working his square jaw beneath his fingers, he looked as though he were suspended in a state of disbelief. "Is she involved?"

"Viva?" Sophia almost laughed over the absurdity of the question. "No, Rook, that's not it. She's seen him with certain people he'd have a challenging time explaining his connection to."

Rook curbed his desire to question further. He knew there was only so much the detective could share. "Why'd you want to see me today?" he asked instead.

Sophia tugged at a lone curl that dangled from her updo and debated before answering. "*I* want to secure V someplace impenetrable until we can convene a grand jury. We don't know if we can indict Dean on what we have now, but we're determined to pull in as much ammunition as we can."

"And you're okay with that? Letting Viva put her ass on the line like this?"

"I don't need my sister to wrap this, Rook." Sophia's voice held the slightest edge. "Viva came to me with this. What she's got to share could tip the scales a lot more in our favor."

"What'd you mean about putting her someplace impenetrable?"

Sophia's shrug momentarily wrinkled her tailored short-waist black blazer. "I'm sure someone in your... line of work would know of such places. You *or* your men," she quickly qualified. "I'm not trying to put you on the spot here, Rook. You could pass this on to one of your guys. Everyone around here will attest to the great work you guys do. I'm at the head of that line. I need to know my sister's someplace safe if she plans on being involved with this thing."

Rook stalked the spacious office, having resumed his jaw massage. He drew to a complete halt at Sophia's next words.

"Tigo said something about you going to Italy."

It seemed that only Rook's facial muscles were capable of movement then. He used them to fix Sophia with a stunned look.

"This all seems so unreal," Veronica Hail cooed while holding her eldest child in a rocking embrace.

Viva enjoyed the feel of being secure in her mother's arms while her father's arms enfolded them both.

"I know this was sudden," Viva said when her parents allowed her to move out of the embrace just a fraction. "Me just showing up out of the blue, but when I heard about Sophia—"

In unison, the Hails were shushing their daughter.

"It's forgotten, baby." Gerald Hail dropped a kiss to the top of Viva's head. "You never have to apologize for coming home."

"You *never had* to apologize."

Viva heard the stress her mother inserted. "Thank you both." She hugged them again. "You guys were right, you know?" She drew back to fix them with solemn looks. "You warned me against jumping for the first brass ring tossed my way. Hmph. I not only jumped, I threw away my future while I did it." Viva saw the look her parents exchanged and read it well.

"I've seen Rook," she told them.

Gerald Hail looked pleased. Veronica Hail looked elated.

"Stop." Viva raised her hands to ward off their glee. "There's no reason to get all crazy happy here. We didn't rush into each other's arms either time."

"Tell us about these 'either times,'" Gerald urged.

The Hails listened intently as Viva recounted the meeting at Sophia's condo days earlier and the party in Sophia's honor the night before.

"Are you sure it means nothing, honey?" Veronica asked.

"I'm sure and it wouldn't matter either way since he's about to head off to Italy." Viva quickly shared the details of Rook's travel plans.

"And how do you feel about this trip?"

Viva shrugged, hesitating to answer her mother's

question. "I'm in no position to complain. I've been out of his life for six years."

"I don't know, Roni, I'm not so sure she answered your question," Gerald Hail teased.

Viva smiled, fought back the urge to laugh. "Hearing him discuss travel plans was like an arrow through my heart. Am I terrible for saying that? *Dramatic* and terrible?"

"Oh well." Gerald squeezed his daughter close and put a kiss to her temple "I'd say yes to the dramatic. You're an actress, after all." He sent her a sly wink. "I don't think we could convict you of being terrible, though."

"Last night, I wished his business deal would fall through so he wouldn't have to go. Sounds pretty terrible to me."

Gerald caught his wife's eye, smiling when she nodded. "I'm gonna go get our coffee, sugar pea. Smells like it's done," he said to Viva after inhaling the air that held the aroma of rich cinnamon.

"Honey, you know you're entitled to have those feelings about the man you love," Veronica was saying once her husband had left the den.

Viva's expression was then playfully stunned. "How do you and Sophia do that? Just assume love is still involved?"

Veronica pulled Viva with her to a time-worn love seat positioned near the fireplace. "I remember that a wedding seemed to be the way things were heading before all those ships started rolling in for you." She put a hand on Viva's knee and squeezed. "You left to follow opportunity, baby, not because you'd fallen out of love with Rook."

"And that has so much to do with it right there. I chucked it all for fame. How shallow could I get?" Viva leaned forward to scrub her face against her palms. "Rook would be an idiot to forget all that and just take me back on faith."

"But would you want him to?"

"He wouldn't, Mama. I'm sure the man certainly has no shortage of women who'd be willing to stay put for anything he'd ask of them." Viva flopped back against the love seat, a dreamy tint softening her eyes. "You should see him, Mama."

"Oh, I have." Veronica gave a coy smile. "So have several of my friends."

The suggestion roused laughter from both women.

"Listen, sugar pea," Veronica said as she slapped Viva's knee then. "There's only one thing wrong with all these women in Rook's perfect life." She tapped her daughter's nose. "He doesn't love any of them, because they aren't you."

"Take her with me? You're serious here?"

"Oh, please stop, Rook." Sophia rolled her eyes. "I've just given you first dibs at an offer every man in the hemisphere would jump to claim."

"She'd never go for it."

Sophia shook her head as if pitying the fact that Rook truly seemed to have no idea of his appeal to the opposite sex. "You know, I'm sure you could find all sorts of ways to persuade her."

"I'm sure I could," Rook said, finally acknowledging a certain level of his power. "But she's also got a job to get back to. Or has her decision to offer testimony against her agent robbed her of her desire to act?"

"She's between projects, and filming for the show won't resume for another five months." She gave him a teasing look. "Are you trying to tell me you're afraid to be alone with a sexy thing like my sister?"

Rook massaged the bridge of his nose and sighed. "You can still be such a brat sometimes."

"I'll have you know that I don't answer to 'brat' anymore, only Chief of Ds." Sophia gave an indignant sniff.

Rook was moved. "I knew you as 'brat' first."

"Level with me, Soap," Rook said once their laughter had eased. "How serious is this? Do you think someone might go after her?"

"I promise you this is only about me erring on the side of caution here." Her gaze turned steely. "No way would I be making jokes and wasting time trying to convince you to do this instead of citing you with some kind of obstruction if you refused to go along." She dismissed the steely look then to make way for one that skirted about playful wickedness.

"I'm leveling with you here, Rook. No way would that be happening if I thought there was any more we should be doing to keep her safe. But I'd still love it if you'd take the job."

Rook worked his fingers against muscles at his nape that had suddenly bunched. "I won't force her to go along with this," he said.

Sophia appeared satisfied. "Don't worry about it. I've got *no* problems with forcing her."

"Please tell me you're calling from Malibu and not back east."

"I'd be happy to tell you that, if you want a lie." Viva grinned at the sound of the familiar nasal voice on the other end of her mobile.

Artesia Relis groaned. "Do you know what you're putting me through here?"

"You mean by visiting my parents for a little TLC?" Viva colored her words with the hint of a snarky undertone.

"Funny." But Artesia didn't sound amused. "I mean leaving us here with Murray. You know no one but you can deal with him when he's riled up."

Viva set down her tanned leather tote bag, deciding to finish the conversation with Murray Dean's assistant there at her parents' place, instead of outside amid steadily dipping temps.

"What's he riled up over?" Viva asked once she'd slipped into the Hails' spacious laundry room. She heard Arty's dramatic sigh—one she'd heard the aspiring actress deliver on countless occasions. Arty had perfected the gesture over the years and it'd become difficult to tell whether the sigh meant true distress or only mild irritation.

"Well, if *you* don't know, how the hell do you think *I* do? I only called because Murray goes back farther with you than anyone." Arty let the sigh make an encore.

"He's been jumpy, snappish and hard to reach. I

mean that literally *and* figuratively, Veev. Half the time, his clients are calling my line because they can't get through to him on his cell. When they do manage to get in touch, they say he's distant. More than a few of his top names are getting nervous and you know what happens when you guys get nervous."

"Yeah…" Viva was working the bridge of her nose between thumb and forefinger. Folks jumped ship when they got nervous. "And you've got no idea what brought this on?" She played the angle, hoping to plumb information Arty may've cast aside.

The practiced sigh made another appearance. "Hard to say… In this business, there's always one thing or another to get pissy over but he did seem more on edge than usual after that meeting a couple of weeks ago."

"Meeting?" Viva peeked out of the laundry room to ensure her privacy was still intact. "Any idea what that was about?"

"Not much. I didn't even have it listed among his appointments. I can tell you they weren't in the business."

"Meaning they weren't actors?"

"Not actors or anyone else connected with the business. They had an…official look about them."

"Cops?" Viva wondered if Sophia had sent investigators to get a feel for their suspect.

"Not sure. I got the feeling their business didn't skirt the right side of the law. Anyway…" Arty's sigh sounded more natural then. "It was just a feeling," she added.

While Viva didn't need the sharp assistant growing suspicious of her questions, she risked one more.

"Do you think you'd recognize them if you saw them again?"

"Sure I would. Veev? Do you think Murray's okay?"

"I'm sure he is, honey. Don't worry, I'll see what I can find out."

"Thanks. Oh, hey! Be on the lookout for that script and the delivery from wardrobe."

"Thanks for the reminder, Art. Hold down the fort and we'll talk soon." Viva ended the connection, waited a beat and then located the number to place a second call. She muttered a curse when she heard the voice-mail greeting.

"Murray? It's Viva. Give me a call, okay?"

Chapter 3

"So these two and these three?" Sophia tapped her fingers to the two-by-three-inch black-and-white mug shots that coincided with her questions.

"Yeah. Those are all I remember from the bunch." Viva leaned back from the small round conference table in her sister's office.

Sophia nodded firmly, looking pleased. Viva had just positively identified the sons of Sylvester Greenway. The construction entrepreneur, and one of their father's oldest friends, had recently come forward with suspicions of his sons' involvement in the money-laundering scheme that had already deposited so many of Philadelphia's finest in holding cells.

Viva's identification of the Greenways was another direct link. Viva had recalled seeing the men at a Malibu party with Murray Dean. The identification added another layer to the case being built around the security-agent-turned-Hollywood-agent-turned-suspected-money-launderer.

Viva watched Sophia remove the book of mug shots. "Is Murray going to jail, Sophia?" she asked after watching her sister quietly for an extended moment.

"It's not a done deal until there's a verdict." Sophia sat on the corner of her big desk. "But a verdict requires a trial first," she said with an encouraging smile for good measure.

"Doesn't seem like I had that much to offer after all."

"Are you kidding? An eyewitness putting Murray with these guys in Cali with the ones here? It's gonna help the DA build an even stronger case. Police work can be a lot of tedious piecing together, but it often results in one colossal wrecking ball at the end."

Viva responded with an airy laugh. "Thanks, Soap, that helps."

"It's the truth." Sophia vacated her spot on the desk and began to browse the files there.

Viva, meanwhile, walked the perimeter of her sister's new and spacious office digs in the heart of downtown. The building, one of Philadelphia's oldest and most stately, boasted offices befitting what the exterior conveyed.

A person with an eye for interior decorating and design, Viva appreciated the efforts taken to ensure Sophia's office was both warm and functional. The formal blackwood paneling and tables of rich cherrywood were softened by suede furnishings of rich earth tones mingled with a few bolder splashes of color that lent the room an efficient yet appropriately chic appearance.

"I can hear your brain over there, but unfortunately I can't translate," Sophia called once silence filled the room for almost two minutes.

Viva turned from the breathtaking wall of windows that presented a glorious view of the city. She looked at her sister who held a handful of folders over a bottom drawer to one side of her desk.

"Is there anything more I could do here, Sophia? Anything more that you'd want me to do?" Viva asked.

Sophia frowned. "Anything more?"

"I called Murray," Viva blurted, knowing that was the only way she could share what she was sure had been a boneheaded move.

Sophia pushed up slowly to stand. "What the hell, V?"

"I didn't want to risk him running, after I talked to his assistant."

"Viva—"

"The girl was at her wits' end when she called, talking about how out of it Murray was acting. She mentioned something about him having a meeting with folks she knew weren't in the business. She said they looked 'official' but she wasn't sure if they were cops or…worse. I thought maybe they could've been cops and I know you can't divulge all the moves you're making in this case, but she said Murray was acting… off ever since and I—I just wanted to help." Viva took a breath following the long spill, winced and waited for the cop in the room to explode.

Sophia stood hunched over the desk. Her hands were splayed across the surface as she inhaled. She straightened, appearing very calm without leaning the slightest bit toward wanting to explode as Viva expected.

"Making sure that a suspect doesn't run isn't your job."

"I was only—" Viva cut herself off, raising her hands in a look of surrender when Sophia's eyes flashed.

"You've done everything I've intended for you to do." Sophia rounded the desk, her expression schooled. "With that in mind, I think it'd be a good idea for you to stay out of sight for a few weeks."

"I agree." Viva began an eager nod, closing some of the distance between her and Sophia. "That won't be a problem at all. The cast has already discussed taking time off to hunker down with the new script for a long rehearsal—"

"Stop." Sophia glared, waiting for Viva to obey. "Staying out of sight means staying *completely* out of sight, away from anywhere Dean might think to look for you if he's got a mind to. Obviously he's got lots of friends in my neck of the woods." She lifted her hands to gesture at their official surroundings. "Ones I've yet to identify. It wouldn't take much for one of them to discover you're on the witness list."

Viva returned to the chair she'd vacated and leaned on the back. "What have you got in mind?"

Sophia propped her hands to her hips, as if preparing for confrontation. "I thought some time out of the country might be a good idea."

"Well, that's great." Viva gave a solitary clap of agreement. "The cast usually does these rehearsal retreats outside the country. We found this really great place when we were on location in the Philippines."

"Viva!" Sophia gave an exasperated sigh. "Completely out of sight means away from your coworkers too."

"Sophia, please tell me you aren't planning to stash me in some old cabin with only cops for company?"

"Oh, I can do way better than that." Sophia gave a flip shrug and went to settle into her comfortable desk chair. "I'm pretty sure you won't be cooped up in an old cabin, but a snowy chalet, and instead of cops, what do you say to a sexy security specialist?"

Sophia's smile sharpened, as did Viva's glare.

"Still can't believe that fool's getting married."

Rook chuckled when Linus Brooks began to laugh. Enjoying the dig at their friend, Linus indulged in a few additional seconds of laughter before helping himself to a swig of the beer Rook had served up from the wall bar in the living area of his office.

"Sophia's a good match for Tig. Always has been." Linus nodded in apparent appreciation of the savory flavor of the chilled imported brew. "Only thing that makes up for the shame of him letting her walk around free all that time is not wasting any more of it before getting her down the aisle."

"Yeah." Rook observed the mug that held his own serving of the beer. "Some fools *do* wise up given enough time."

As Rook prowled the length of the tall windows behind his desk he felt Linus's eyes on him. "Lotta mess went down between them, but…if *they* could work it out…" Linus trailed off as Rook fixed him with a look. "I'd take that to mean it's never too late, is all I'm saying."

"I'm on my way to Italy in a week," Rook said in a manner to rival the softness of the rain tapping his office window that afternoon.

"A lot could happen in a week," Linus said.

"Not that."

"Rook—"

"Sophia and Tig made a mess of things, but at least they had the time and space to fix it." Briefly, Rook closed his eyes to the dreary view. "How are we ever to fix anything when she's halfway around the world or across the country?"

"Last I heard, *you* were your own boss." Undeterred, Linus swigged down another gulp of the beer. "Educate me on exactly what's stopping you."

"Do you really need me to go into that?" Despite the amount of beer he'd downed, Rook's throat still felt as scratchy as a square of sandpaper.

Understanding pooled in Linus's ebony eyes. "Do you want her back?"

"I never wanted her to go."

"She's here now."

"She is…" Rook seemed to consider the simple truth, but only momentarily. "Trying to work this out with Viva will be messy, Linus. People change and six years is a long time."

The cool understanding on Linus's sculpted dark face meshed with empathy. "You're not a victim to that anymore."

"But it's still in me." Rook tapped the bottom of his mug to a denim-clad knee once he'd taken a seat in front of his desk. "Isn't that what we're always supposed to remember? That it would always be inside us, lurking?" He looked to Linus. "That what we have to focus on now is managing it because we'll never be rid of it?"

With a nod he appeared reluctant to give, Linus set aside his beer. Rook tilted back more of his, knowing he didn't need to say more. Linus understood. After all, Rook reminisced, it had been his old friend who had recognized the signs of Rook's anger morphing into an uncontrollable monster inside him.

It had been Linus who'd bravely forged ahead. He'd refused to let Rook's increasingly hostile mood spook him into doing nothing to help him find the means to battle the darkness carving a spot inside him.

"I don't want her to see that in me."

"You'd never hurt her."

"I know that." Rook's tone was black, yet with a matter-of-fact tinge. "Doesn't mean I want her to see me launch a TV through a plate-glass window because I was aggravated over some ancient drama."

"Might do you both some good. Not tossing a TV through plate glass," Linus clarified with a laugh when Rook glared. "I mean getting this poison out of your system. Finally telling her how what she did made you feel."

Rook shook his head stubbornly. "She wasn't to blame."

"I didn't say she was, but what happened put you in a real bad place—a place you haven't all the way come back from." Linus came to take a chair closest to the one Rook occupied. "You'll never truly manage this crap if you don't share some of that weight with her. Do that at least—even if nothing more comes of it. She'll head back to California and you'll make your moves, but you'll make 'em without a lot of weight from the past dragging at you and dangling like a carrot in front of that monster you need to control."

"Does Eli know you moonlight as a shrink?" Rook teased, referring to Elias Joss, another of their friends and Linus's business partner.

"Aw, he's used to it." Linus gave a playful eye roll. "'Specially if it means the happiness of a friend.

"Look, man," Linus said once laughter was shared. "The last thing I want is for everything you've got pent up to barrel out unexpectedly. Trust me, I know what the consequences of that feels like."

Rook spread his big hands. "What? Am I giving off some kind of dark vibe?"

"No, but I know Viva being back has to be adding some kind of pressure. That added to the fact that you've missed two meetings…and now you're about to take a long trip… Well, I'm a little concerned."

"Don't be." Rook leaned over to slap at Linus's forearm beneath the fleece sleeve of his sweatshirt. "I'm good. I've been good. No reason to think that won't continue."

The phone rang and both men grinned as though the sound were a good omen.

"Yeah, Lind?" Rook greeted his assistant Lindy Peters, by speaker.

"Sorry, Rook, I thought you'd want to take this call. It's Chief Hail."

Linus left his chair, taking his empty beer mug which he used to motion to Rook for another refill.

Rook nodded, appreciating the bit of privacy. "Send

her through." In a few seconds he heard the click on the line. "Soap? Linus is here."

"Hey, Linus!" Sophia called through the speaker.

Rook silenced the speaker once Linus sent his greetings. As Linus busied himself browsing the extensive stock of domestic and imported beers behind the bar, Rook listened to what Sophia had to say. His responses into the phone turned shorter and he couldn't keep frustration from creeping into his voice. Linus must have heard it too, because he returned to his chair and offered an encouraging shrug when the call ended.

"Scratch everything I just said," Rook ordered his friend.

"Viva?"

Her hands going still on the straps of an enormous tan tote bag, Viva turned toward the sound of the vaguely familiar voice that was presently etched with curiosity. Laughter tickled her throat when she saw Burt Larkin standing in the doorway of Rook's office.

"So is it all right to be here in the control room?" Viva asked once she and Burt had exchanged hugs and pleasantries. "Rook's assistant told me to come on in."

"You're fine and besides, it's the best place for you." Burt scratched at a wheat-colored brow. "How'd you get in here without being mobbed anyway?"

Viva gave her tote bag a shake. "Never underestimate the power of a good wig and sunglasses. Sophia told me how to get here but my guess is she regrets that now after ordering me to go along with Rook putting his life on hold to babysit me. I'm sure you know about that."

Burt nodded. "I may've heard something, but I'm sure he doesn't see it as babysitting and putting his life on hold, Viva."

"I'm here to see that he does."

Viva's practiced bravado threatened mutiny when she saw Rook arriving at his office door.

"So I'm gonna head out," Burt said, putting a knowing smile in place. He went to pull Viva into a quick, warm embrace. "Have someone find me before you leave, so I can get an autograph. It'll make me the envy of all my playmates."

"Promise!" Viva laughed.

Burt kept the smile on his attractively weather-beaten face when he sidestepped his boss.

Rook shut the door at Burt's back and was facing it when he began to speak to Viva. "Sophia called, said you might stop by."

"Wow." Viva set aside her tote bag and pretended to be impressed. "Calls announcing my arrival...you and Sophia sure are close these days."

Rook strolled to his desk, which was a fixture of gleaming blackwood in the back of the spacious yet efficient office. Rook allowed himself few comforts when he worked. Even the well-stocked bar and living area radiated Spartan undertones.

"Chief of Ds thinks me and my team do a pretty decent job."

"I'm sure that's true, but you don't need to waste your resources on me."

"Last thing it'd be is a waste." Rook settled onto one corner of the broad, neat desk. "There's no need for a large crew. This is a one-man job."

"Rook, I'm sorry." Viva stopped a few feet before him at the desk.

"Sorry?" He tensed. "What for?"

"Sophia should've never pulled you into this."

"And why is that?" Rook faked a little confusion. "I supply security and you're obviously in need of it."

Viva eased her hands into the side pockets of the teal skirt that showcased her curves and shapely calves where the hem ended just below the knee. "Just what did Sophia tell you?" Suspicion was rife in her slightly husky voice.

"Not much." Rook studied his hands while he rubbed his palms. "Enough to give me a sense of what's going on, but I suspect she's leaving it up to you to share all the…colorful details." He treated himself to a brief but effective appraisal of her body that she felt in every nerve ending. "Sophia gave me the feeling there were several," he added when her eyes met his again.

I'll bet she did, Viva mused silently, feeling the crushing need to act on her threats of bodily harm to her little sister.

Rook made a pretense of straightening the few files lying on his pristine desk. "I've got time to talk now if you want."

"Rook," Viva began in a manner that rarely failed to get her what she wanted. "Listen, I—I don't want you involved with this and I'd appreciate you going to Soap and telling her to put someone else on it."

"No." The response was quick, cold. Rook didn't even spare Viva a glance as he studied the paperwork on his desk.

Viva wasn't surprised by the answer; she knew it'd

been useless to ask the question. She'd only been using the "get me what I want" voice since her name had become a recognizable one. It had proved a successful technique—on most everyone except her sister. Trying it with Rook was just as idiotic. When safety was an issue, he was deaf to any attempt at making light of it.

"So what about your trip to Italy?" she asked then, minus the "get me what I want" emphasis.

"What about it?" He gave her the benefit of his gaze then.

"Are you still going?"

"Yes."

Viva took a quiet moment to process. "Well, how can you do that and watch *me* 24/7?"

He smiled. "I can do that because you're going with me. I'm sure Sophia told you that already."

"I can't."

"You will."

"You'll force me?"

"I've been promised that I won't have to."

"Sophia." Viva hissed her sister's name like it was a curse. "So you already know this involved Murray." She decided it wouldn't hurt to come clean—a little.

Rook tilted his head a fraction, no doubt hoping to shield the sudden and fanatical twitch of a jaw muscle. It was a futile attempt. "I know that."

"And you expect us to just go off to Italy together without that being a problem for us?"

Infuriatingly cool then, Rook leaned forward a tad. "I don't expect that at all," he told her.

"Then what?"

"I expect you to tell me whatever your sister suspects you're keeping from me."

Viva couldn't resist a quick burst of laughter. "What she *suspects* I'm keeping? You're going off the assumption that her suspicions are correct."

"She's a cop. A damn good one. *So* good, she got a promotion most cops don't even bother to dream about at her age." He shrugged. "Yeah, I'm good with assuming her suspicions are correct."

"And did she give you any hints about what she suspects?"

"No. My guess is she's hoping you'll use the time to get into it."

Viva moved closer, resting a hip on the desk when she faced him. "You know she wants me protected because of Murray's involvement with her case."

"I know." A muscle danced wickedly in his cheek. "That alone is enough to make me want in on this."

"And you don't expect this trip to give you any stress and headaches you don't need while you're trying to get your business in order?"

"I expect this trip will give me *a lot* of stress and headaches I don't need, but you're crazy if you think I'd say no to this, V."

With a sigh, Viva studied the low, yet cushioned dark carpeting beneath her pumps. "Rook, you should know that I called Murray. I left a message for him to get in touch. His assistant says he's been acting weird and she thought I could talk him down." Viva thought she saw the carpet blur before her eyes as the explanation spilled out. "I thought it'd be a good idea to call, so he wouldn't run."

Rook watched her like she'd sprouted a second head. "What the hell did you think you were doing?"

"Spare me the lecture," Viva retorted with an airy

wave and eye roll. "Sophia beat you to it and then ordered me to go along with whatever you say. Do you have any idea how frustrating it is to have your baby sister giving you orders like that?"

Rook only grunted a low curse while flexing a fist. "We leave on Thursday," he said.

"Thursday? But that barely gives me time to—" She silenced at the look he sent her way.

"Rook," she pleaded then, hunching over the desk and spreading her hands across the gleaming surface. "See reason here. Murray's my agent. I can't just disappear. What am I supposed to tell him if he calls me back?"

"Do you really want me to answer that?" Rook's insanely desirable face was a study in pure menace.

"Well, I have to tell him something." Viva blew at a curl that bounced between her brows. "He practically has to beg me to take breaks. He'd never believe I just ran off and—"

"Not even if you told him you ran off with me?"

Openmouthed, Viva could only stare.

Rook took advantage of the quiet. "Tell him we're rekindling the flame. Tell him…tell him I threatened to tie you to my bed until you agreed to go along and you believed me. I think that's a threat I've followed through on a time or two, isn't it?"

Viva tried to speak, laugh, something…but she failed at every attempt. She ran her tongue over her lips and tried speaking again. "He'd know that's not true. He'd know I'm lying—"

Any further argument was silenced once he kissed her and her tongue was otherwise engaged with his. Rook had taken command of her wrist and tugged her across the brief space separating them on the desk. Seamless and confident, he settled her across the broad width of his thigh, making her straddle the limb in a ruthless, brazen manner.

The stretchy fabric of her skirt eased up to accommodate the change in her position. Viva didn't care that his manner was raw and hungry so long as he didn't stop. She wasted no time snuggling into the kiss. It was hers to enjoy...or resist.

There was but subtle command at the heart of the way he held her. He was giving her the chance to resist if she wanted, but resistance was light-years away from Viva's consciousness. Nothing could make her withdraw from the wondrous soothing sensation of his tongue stroking and loving her mouth in a way that only *he* could.

Rook apparently felt differently and began to withdraw from the kiss. He didn't leave her cold. Instead, the heated strokes of his tongue cooled to adopt a lazier pace, until he was running the tip along her teeth and the velvety softness of her bottom lip. Then he was kissing her there, pampering the area with whisper-soft, sugary pecks that had her moaning in want of more.

Viva kept her eyes closed, when there was no further pressure against her mouth. She hoped the stimulating pecks—at the very least—would resume. There was nothing. She opened her eyes then, wondering if he felt the thud of her heart as she drowned in the radiance of his amber stare.

Rook used only his thumb to caress her mouth. He smiled, appreciating the unsmudged quality of her petal-pink lipstick. Then he returned his gaze to hers.

"Now you won't have to lie," he said.

Viva let out the breath she hadn't realized she was holding and tried to speak his name. She failed. Gently, Rook set her back where she was.

"Thursday," he said and then left her to head behind his desk.

Swamped by a haze of confusion and unquenched need, Viva managed to snap to. She collected some of her scattered nerves and just managed to leave the room without tripping over herself.

Chapter 4

Tamping down her uneasiness took more time than Viva expected—a thing she realized when she headed out of Rook's office and took the elevator down to the mezzanine level in search of a less direct route outside. From there, it was a short walk down a wide staircase boxed in glossy dark oak and down a set of stairs to the lobby.

The elevator descent and stroll from the mezzanine had proved uneventful enough. That changed when she stepped out into L Sec's bustling switchboard division. Collecting scattered nerves hadn't left her time to remember her disguise.

A surreal moment of uninterrupted quiet set in amongst the inhabitants of the switchboard hub as Viva looked over the once-busy staff. Seconds passed and then the stirrings of hushed conversation eased in like a mist over quiet. The hushed conversation gained volume as acknowledgment took hold. Once the first courageous soul approached the well-known actress, pandemonium ensued.

Despite frazzled nerves, Viva laughed. She didn't mind the attention. She adored her fans. She'd relied on their adoration to pull her out of depressive bouts when they struck more often than she could count.

Signing autographs while making her way through the lobby to the main entrance took all of eighty minutes. Beyond the skyscraper's towering doors, she practically speed-walked to her rental car and fumbled with the key to deactivate the locks. She slipped into the driver's seat, expelling a relieved whoosh of breath once she was concealed behind the car's darkly tinted windows.

The soothing medley of wind chimes gave her cause to jump as her nerves still proved to be unsettled from the kiss. Viva laughed over the self-criticism. It was a kiss, true, but there was no such thing as *only* a kiss when Rook Lourdess was the supplier. Besides… she'd gone without his kisses for far too long.

The phone chimed again and she forced her attention to the screen. Another jolt attacked her senses when her agent's name floated into view.

Closing her eyes, Viva instinctively forced aside all distractions and put herself in character to accept the call. "Hey, Murray," she greeted him in the voice of airy delight that had become her trademark.

"Veev, what's up, love? Everything all right?"

Viva hesitated on her response. She hadn't expected him to ask how she was given how distracted she'd heard he'd been.

"Well, you know how it is… I've been a little out of it lately." She played along, hoping it might encourage him to open up.

"Guess it's weird going home after all this time, huh?"

Viva's smile held a poignant gleam. "Weird, but good," she admitted.

"Glad to hear it." Murray's voice seemed to hold a similar poignancy.

"So are *you* okay? You sound a little drained."

"I am."

"Business?" Viva straightened a little on the suede seat of the sporty BMW. She knew he'd take her query about business to understand that she was referring to show business.

"The outskirts of the business."

"Talk to me, Murray." His distinction encouraged her to probe a little deeper.

Murray evidently needed to vent. "Seems I've got some associates who've decided to try smearing my name."

"Murray, that's terrible. What's going on? Is there anything I can do?"

"Sweet thing—" Murray chuckled "—this is nothing you need to worry your fine self over. I've got it under control. They'll shut their mouths sooner or later. So, um…how's Sophia?"

Viva blinked. "Sophia? Um, fine, fine, she's great. Getting married."

"Ahh, marriage *and* a promotion."

"You—you heard about that all the way out west?"

"News travels, Veev, and I make a point to keep up

with what's goin' on back home, you know? I heard she was working on some money-laundering thing."

"Yeah, she, um…she's close to wrapping it up, actually." Viva debated momentarily and then continued, "She's already made some big arrests. Looks like a winner for her."

"Sounds like she's on top of it."

Viva leaned back on the headrest. "Guess that's why she got the big promotion."

"Mmm…" Murray's silence hung on the line for several seconds. "So how long are you planning to be back east?"

"Not long, actually, um, that's why I called." She cast a quick look across the parking lot in the direction of L Sec. "I'm heading off on another trip, Mur. Just wanted to tell you before I left and to make sure we could stay in touch. I didn't know if you had any big plans or not."

"So where are you heading off to?"

Viva paused for dramatic effect. "I've, um… I've seen Rook since I've been home."

Murray's insightful "mmm…" hit the air again. "Doesn't surprise me, Veev. Even after all this time, there's still a lot of unfinished business between you guys. Makes sense Rook wouldn't want to let any more time pass after doing nothing to stop you from leaving before."

"Murray, stop. The blame isn't all on Rook."

"You're right. You're right, and I hope things work out. You guys got a bad break back then."

"Thank you, Murray." She was genuinely surprised by his words. "Murray, are you gonna be okay? Is there anything I can do?"

"Nothing. Like I said—I'll be fine. There're just some things I need to tidy up. You can call my personal cell if you need to reach me." He chuckled. "You think Rook will let you take calls once he whisks you away?"

Viva was laughing softly. "I'm sure. Jeez, Murray, I'm so on edge about the whole thing...just be available if I call and need to vent."

"You can count on me, Veev, don't worry." Murray was laughing then, but his voice had chilled. "Everything'll be fine once I put some stuff to bed."

The call ended shortly after with goodbyes and more laughter. Viva kept the phone to her ear and turned Murray's words over in her mind. She didn't spend much time on the endeavor, realizing she didn't really want to know what they meant.

Viva's nerves had settled by the time she'd returned to her sister's. When she'd arrived in Philadelphia, Sophia had said there was no reason for her to get a hotel room. As the two of them would be spending most nights talking until the wee hours anyway, they may as well do that someplace more like home.

Viva could've really used Sophia's ear when she arrived at the condo from Rook's office.

Thankfully, her sister was but a phone call away—a fact Viva took advantage of once she'd set aside her disguise bag and changed into loungewear. She contacted Sophia and they rehashed Murray's call while Viva took the edge off the day by indulging in a few glasses of wine.

"Did it sound like he was still in California?" Sophia asked.

Viva swirled the wine in her amber-colored glass and smiled as Rook's similarly colored eyes came to mind. "I couldn't get a sense of where he was."

"'Putting stuff to bed.' That's an odd phrase..." Sophia seemed to be considering that bit of info.

"Yeah, that part freaked me out too." Viva rested back on the sofa, knees raised and bared when the hem of the lounge dress hiked up. "I never heard him talk that way. What do you think it means?"

"Sounds ominous, that's for sure...like maybe he's planning to silence those who could be a threat to him. Do you get it now why I need you to stay out of sight? Murray knows there've been arrests, but he's still set on 'putting stuff to bed,' which could mean he's got more partners out there lurking who could still do damage."

"I get it, Soap," Viva drawled as she downed a bit more of the wine.

"It's just that I've still got folks in my own organization I can't trust," Sophia continued. "I just need you to understand that being with Rook is the safest place you can be."

"I know, Sophia, I know." Viva closed her eyes and rested her head back on the sofa.

"So you went to see Rook, huh?" Sophia asked once another wave of silence hit.

"I tried to talk him out of watching over me."

"I didn't have to twist his arm about doing it, you know. He won't rest until he knows you're safe."

"Yeah." Viva helped herself to another generous swallow of the dry white. "He kissed me," she blurted shortly after.

Sophia gasped and then coughed. "You cold wench! How the hell could you tell me that over the phone?"

"Tried to wait," Viva said as she yawned. "Figured I'd be too wasted to make any sense by the time you got home."

"Well, dammit, stop drinking. I'm on my way."

"He threatened to tie me to his bed if I didn't go along with your plan. I've been tied to Rook's bed before, Soap."

"Mmm...I see. I take it that's a threat you'd want him to make good on?"

"God, yes."

Sophia muttered a playful curse into the phone. "Stop drinking. I'll be there soon."

The connection broke in Viva's ear. "Sure thing," she drawled into the dead receiver. "Soon as I have just a little more." She finished the wine, reached for the half-empty bottle and poured another glass.

"Well, if it ain't the bridegroom!" Rook called to Santigo when he saw him heading for Sophia's condo building around sunset. "Congratulations again, man," he said when they met for handshakes and hugs.

"Time heals all wounds," Tigo said, his darkly handsome face alive with humor and happiness.

Rook winced. "So I keep hearing."

"Well, the statement could stand a little tweaking, I guess," Tigo contemplated aloud. "How about this—wounds heal best when folks stop jabbing at each other."

"Ah...so that's where we've been screwing up."

"Is that 'we' as in you and Viva?"

"Come off it, Tig," Rook said as he and Tigo scanned

their IDs at the sensor just next to the bay of revolving glass doors. "I know your fiancée clued you in to all my new drama."

"Not really. We really haven't had much time together." Tigo slipped his ID into his wallet and appeared playfully crestfallen. "Not much time to get into anything dramatic. Thank God." He grinned.

Rook reciprocated the gesture and appreciated his friend's joy. "Hate to break it to you, but I'm sure that's about to change."

Tigo's steps slowed and he turned. "Anything you wanna just go on and tell me?"

Rook worked the bridge of his nose between thumb and forefinger. "Sophia wants Viva to come with me to Italy."

Tigo whistled. "Jeez, man, that's putting a new spin on business and pleasure."

"Tell me about it."

Both men wore genuine smiles when they paused to greet residential security. The guards in the pine-and-glass-encased booth were especially friendly as they recognized their boss. The men chatted for a while. Tigo took time out to let Sophia know he was there and who he was with. Appreciating the heads-up, Sophia asked them to give her and Viva time to spruce up the place before they came up.

"Looks like L Sec's movin' in," Tigo noted once they were moving beyond the booth toward the elevator bay.

"Looks like." Rook shrugged, his expression reflecting satisfaction. "The building's owners got concerned after what happened to Sophia. They thought they could stand to put more security in place for their residents." He gestured to the ceiling where a magnificent skylight directed weak late-autumn sunlight into the lobby. "Everyone around here seems to like the changes. It's made your wife-to-be a popular girl."

"So are you really good with this—taking V along with you?" Tigo asked once their laughter had eased. "Soap'll understand if it's too much with all that's happened."

Rook leaned against an opposing wall while Tigo hit the button for the elevator. "I know I'm a fool to go along with it, but..." He mopped his face in his palms.

Tigo grinned. "I get it, man. So do you think you guys'll be back for the wedding?"

Rook pushed off the wall. "You guys set a date already?"

"Done wasting time," Tigo said matter-of-factly. "We don't need some huge, crazy event. Right now, we're working to get the folks to go along with that." He laughed. "Guess I've got some drama goin' after all."

"The good kind." Rook clapped Tigo's shoulder as they stepped into an arriving elevator car.

"You want Viva back?" Tigo asked when the car's paneled doors closed with a muffled thud.

"More than anything." Rook relaxed against the paneling and closed his eyes. "And before you say it, yes, I know time isn't on our side."

"There are really only two things you need to ask yourself," Tigo said as he leaned on the wall next to Rook. "Is it worth it and does she feel the same?"

"Do you mean in the physical or mental sense?" Rook's sly smile mimicked his tone of voice. "I can tell you I don't have a clue where her head is."

"So handle your business in Italy and do what you need to in order to settle this between you and V."

Rook gave his old friend a sideways glance. "You know, you're starting to sound like Linus."

"Is that good or bad?"

Laughter filled the ascending car.

"Jeez, V, why couldn't you just listen to me for once in your life? Just believe your little sister knows what she's talking about?" Sophia grumbled when she rushed back into the living room from the kitchen where she'd started a pot of coffee and deposited Viva's emptied wine bottle.

Sophia stooped before Viva, whom she'd found dozing when she got home. She gave her big sister's cheek a quick, light slap. "Come on, girl, the guy of your dreams is on his way up. This is no time for you to be playing the role of the drunken lush.

"V?" She slapped Viva's cheeks again. "Do you hear me?" she queried when her sister groaned. "He's on his way up."

Rousted a bit, Viva's eyes opened to narrow slits. "Up?"

"Rook's coming up."

Viva groaned.

"Come on, V." Sophia added a few more taps to her sister's face.

Viva winced. "You're just doing that to be mean now."

"You know me so well." Sophia pushed to her feet. "Don't go back to sleep!" she called, heading back to the kitchen to check on the coffee. "Locks are off the door, so Rook and Tigo can come on in!"

Viva cradled her head, resting her elbows on her knees as she groaned anew. "Why'd you ask him over?"

"I didn't." Sophia stepped out of the kitchen to answer. "Maybe he wanted to come check and see how you were recovering from that kiss he laid on you earlier."

"You're not helping."

"You'll be okay," Sophia crooned. "You've got several weeks of lavish Italian living coming to you."

"I know what you're doing."

"Oh, yeah? What am I doing?" Sophia returned to the living room with a loaded coffee tray in tow. "Looks like I'm slaving to fix you coffee even after the day I've had." She set down the tray and sighed. "This is why people hate celebrities."

Viva's expression was bland. "People don't hate celebrities."

"They do when they have to deal with 'em in real life."

Viva's misery fully reasserted itself then. "Why couldn't he put up this much effort when I first left?"

"You wouldn't have heard what he had to tell you then." Sophia poured the delicious-smelling brew into an oversize glazed mug depicting a fall scene.

"How do you know that?" Viva tried to pout.

"I know that because I knew you then," Sophia replied as she added cream to the strong black coffee until it turned to an inviting rich beige. "The only thing you loved more than Rook Lourdess was the acting bug."

"So this is my fault?"

"Your words, not mine." Sophia pushed the mug

into Viva's hands. "Drink this." She nodded as her instructions were followed and then moved to prepare her own cup.

"V, we could go back and forth on this all day and into next year, but you only need to remember one thing. Be honest with him." Sophia blew across the surface of the coffee, took a sip and smiled in appreciation of the taste.

"Just tell him whatever it is you think he won't understand," she continued. "You're already apart. There's nothing to lose now, is there?"

Viva started to take another sip of her coffee, but paused. "How easy was all that 'honesty is the best policy' stuff before you and Tig worked it out?"

Sophia savored more of her coffee, her glee apparent in the contented smile and happy shiver she gave. "I never went through anything so hard in my whole life. It wasn't easy—it was hell. Felt like I was walking on coals a lot of the time."

Viva rolled her eyes. "Thanks," she said flatly.

"Anytime." Sophia sipped more coffee and then sighed when she heard a knock at the door.

"I told Tigo to just come on in."

"Why do you keep throwing us together?" Viva set her mug to the stone table before the sofa while Sophia stood to answer the knock. "Do you know how long it's taken me to get over that man?"

Sophia paused a few feet from the door. "I don't know. Why don't you tell me when it happens?"

"I hate you."

Sophia laughed. "You love me."

Chapter 5

"You should've called again," Rook suggested to Tigo once they'd stepped into the condo and saw Viva resting back on the sofa, an arm thrown over her eyes in a picture of woe.

"She started the party without us," Sophia explained as she reclaimed her coffee mug from an end table.

Rook was already kneeling next to the sofa and cupping Viva's jaw. "Is she okay?"

"I'm fine," Viva slurred.

Rook looked to the coffee mug and then gave Viva's jaw a little squeeze. "Didn't you tell your sister that stuff does nothing to perk you up?"

Viva responded with a lazy smile. "It's a cop thing. Coffee's their go-to cure for whatever ails you."

In retaliation, Sophia yanked her sister's hair as she walked past. Tigo soothed the gesture, when Viva cried out, with a kiss to his soon-to-be sister-in-law's brow.

Rook chuckled as the couple headed into the kitchen. "I just wanted to check on you," he told her.

Viva's smile refreshed. "Why? Did you think I'd pass out from the strength of one kiss?"

Rook fingered away the tip of a curl clinging to the corner of her mouth. "It's been known to happen," he said. "Will you let me take you to bed?"

"Mmm…yes…" she purred without hesitation. Instantly she regretted the slip and silently bemoaned the fact that coffee really had no effect on her.

Rook moved in, easily taking her into his arms. "Let's go, I know something that'll work better than coffee."

"Sex?" Viva's tone was hopeful.

Rook laughed. "Sleep."

"I sleep better after sex." She figured she'd already done a fine job of putting her foot in her mouth. No sense stopping now.

Rook played the game in stride. Inside, he wished she'd shut up. In that moment, all he could think of was putting her to bed…with sex. "You already had the wine to help with that," he managed to say.

Viva merely smiled and let her head rest on his shoulder. She enjoyed the security coursing through her in reaction to the broad expanse of muscle supporting her head. Sleepily, she gave him directions to her room.

"Rook," she murmured into his neck, "I miss you."

He grinned then, taking her confession to be alcohol-induced. "I miss you too," he said, playing along. He felt her mouth against his seconds later.

He had no thought to question whether the gesture was alcohol induced or not. He had no thoughts, period—save the fact that they were engaged in a kiss. The second one in over six years.

Somehow, he found the way to her room. One kick from his boot secured the door and sealed them in a cocoon of darkness inside. Rook made no effort to venture any farther beyond the door. He stood, holding her high and close to his chest as the kiss grew more heated and urgent.

The kiss had begun sweetly enough with Viva's lazy exploration of his mouth. Her tongue had grazed his even teeth before curling sensually around his tongue. Now though it turned potent, and Rook's groans mingled with the soft, infectious purrs of pleasure stirring in the back of her throat. Her firm breasts were more than a handful and for that, Rook had no complaints. His only regret was that they weren't filling his hands just then. Cursing raggedly to himself, he drove his tongue against hers.

He moved forward, hoping the bed wasn't too far away. He felt the edge of the mattress nudging him a moment later.

Viva could feel herself lowering and instinctively curved her fingers about his open shirt collar. She was determined to take him down with her.

Rook needed no encouragement on that score. He caged her beneath his wide frame, never once breaking the kiss as he settled between her thighs. The satiny limbs had been bared by the rising hem of the ankle-length lounge dress she wore.

Viva could only gasp when she felt his arousal. His erection was stiffly pronounced, appreciatively wedged against the dampened middle of her panties. Her back bowed as she arched, rubbing against Rook in an attempt to ease away the ache stirred by him there so close to the spot he had been the first to awaken and possess.

It was a possession he still held claim to, Viva admitted in the quiet of her mind. Time had not erased what he and he alone could make her feel with a look or the slightest touch.

There was nothing *slight* about his touch then, however. His crushing weight was a welcome pressure against her body—one that had been so very missed during the six-year drought of their separation. She arched and rubbed against him more insistently. Simultaneously, she engaged her breasts in the lusty interlude.

It was impossible for Rook to ignore the plump mounds crushing into his chest with burgeoning persistence. His palms literally ached with the need to feel the nipples naked against his skin. Yet he resisted, knowing if he indulged, he wouldn't be leaving her until the morning, if then. Clenching his fists, Rook launched an attempt to ease away, to withdraw from the kiss and the haze of pleasure only she had the power to lock him in.

Viva wasn't the least on board with calling a halt to their moment. Her nails grazed the short, cottony waves tapering his nape in a play to keep him close. Even as she continued to move her breasts across his chest, she was freeing her hold at his nape to tug at the ties securing the bodice of her dress.

Rook latched onto the dredges of his willpower and shook his head as he withdrew. "No, V..."

She responded by clutching fistfuls of his shirt and rocking her hips with deliberate insistence. "You don't mean it."

"Damn right, I don't, but it needs to be said."

She gave a throaty laugh, one he'd missed hearing in his ear. Until then, he'd only been able to enjoy the sound from an impersonal distance through a TV or movie screen.

Viva resumed her sweet rocking and the moves had Rook stiffening then to an almost painful state. He surprised them both when he wrenched back. Capturing Viva's wrists, he pressed them above her head, before she could snag his shirt again.

In the weak streams of the streetlights fighting their way past the blinds, he saw her face. The disappointment in her expression broke his heart and for an instant, his temper flared at the idea of her gracing any other man with that look. That look that could render a man incapable of denying her anything. That look that had the power to caress a man's ego, bolster his pride and reduce him to a sex-starved mess all in the same vein.

Considering the idea of her giving that look to another was time poorly spent. That was doubly true for a man currently working to keep a tight rein on his anger. He kissed her sweetly then—a peck to each eyelid. He smiled, noting that she couldn't quickly open them following the kisses, as if they were still weighted down by exhaustion.

"Get some sleep," he murmured next to her ear.

"Stay," she urged.

"I'm not going anywhere," he promised her and realized that he meant it.

"So you're sure your dirty coworkers are as safe as they can be?"

Sophia had just told Rook and Santigo about Viva's call with Murray Dean.

"They're locked up tight," Sophia responded to Rook's question from her snug spot against Tigo on the sofa. "But Murray's words do give us more to consider, like who he might have on the inside that could make my dirty coworkers *less* safe and who we've yet to lock away or put into protective custody before he can 'put them to bed' as he said."

"Hell," Tigo groaned. "How does an agent get tied up in something like this? I mean, I know Hollywood isn't filled with the most angelic souls, but money laundering and using gentlemen's clubs and dirty cops in the mix is quite a stretch."

"The guy was always ambitious," Rook said from his relaxed position in a suede recliner across the room. "Murray wanted the shine and he wasn't above doing what he had to, to get it. Even if it meant pinching off something someone else had already put together."

"Murray worked for you back in the day, right?" Tigo asked.

Rook's nod was a grim confirmation. "He jumped ship without notice to establish his own security firm. Then he added insult to injury when he tried to make off with my staff."

"He's a bold criminal. You have to give him that," Sophia mused.

"You guys think he could've been into all this back then?" Tigo asked.

Rook was first to speak up. "He was ambitious, but I never saw anything that rang criminal."

"They rang unethical though," Sophia said as she shrugged beneath the plum scoop-neck top she'd worn with her blazer that day. "From there, it's not always the biggest leap to the criminal side of things.

"Guess it couldn't hurt to check into what Mr. Dean's got going on behind the scenes on a personal level financially," Sophia suggested once silence held for a time. "Property holdings and things of that nature could provide heavy incentive for certain unethical acts. We've been looking at his current acts, but it could pay to see if our friendly neighborhood agent was living above his legal means and for how long."

"I should've stopped her from going with him." Rook had left the recliner and was pacing. His habitual fist clenching had once again taken hold.

"Easy, man," Tigo soothed. "How could you have known it'd go down this way?"

"I knew," Rook responded blackly. "I probably knew long before Murray pulled his disappearing act and tried to take half my team along for the ride. I should've known something."

"Well, we can change that now." Sophia eased from Tigo's comforting embrace to study Rook. "When this all hits the fan, you can believe Murray's going to be reaching out to all his contacts to rally in defense of his good name. Viva will be right at the top of that list."

"Damn if I let that happen," Rook grumbled, sliding an acid look toward the hallway leading to the bedrooms.

"You're welcome to stay," Sophia told him, no doubt following the path of his glare. "That room's big enough for two."

Her nonsubtle attempt drew a smile to Rook's mouth and he fixed her with a sly look. "How can you be such a dynamic cop and have such a problem stopping yourself from being so obvious?"

Sophia settled back against Tigo. "When I see travesties, I pull out all the stops to get them corrected."

"Understood, and I love you for trying." Rook eased a haunted look toward the hallway again. "It's gonna take more to correct this than us being in the same place at the same time. I don't know if either of us is ready for a discussion of how many ways we've screwed up." He shook his head as if to clear it, turned and crossed to the sofa where he dropped a kiss to Sophie's forehead.

"Tell her I'll see her tomorrow," Rook instructed while shaking hands with Tigo. He only nodded at the concern he saw in the couple's eyes before he left.

"Yeah, this is gonna go over real well... I'll spend half the season recovering from a broken leg," Viva grumbled the next morning while giving a skeptical look to the shoe she held.

The studio that produced the cable crime drama that she'd been a part for the last five years had delivered the script for the new season. The wardrobe department had also included a package with the shipment. The spike-heeled pump she held would've easily added at least six inches to her height.

After unpacking about eight pairs of the chic stems, Viva began an immediate scan of the script to determine what the writers had in store for her tough and usually no-nonsense character. Apparently, a new undercover assignment would require her to saunter around in the bona fide neck breakers over the course of several episodes.

Viva had nothing against fierce footwear, but filming could last several weeks and hours on end each day. Flouncing around in stilts for much of that time wasn't her idea of a fun work environment. With a resolved, albeit grim smile, Viva slipped into a pair of the intimidating pumps, bracing herself on the boxy arms of the chair she occupied before standing.

Though pumps were familiar staples of her wardrobe, she did exercise a fair amount of discernment when it came to the potential for breaking her behind all in the name of fashion.

"Anyway..." she groaned, taking a tentative step. "For the fans..."

The shoes were to die for, she thought. Pink satin inlaid on white leather straps that crossed over the top of the shoe. The material seemed to glimmer when it captured the light.

Despite the killer height, the shoes felt remarkably comfortable. Viva didn't know if it was her familiarity with heels or that the shoes really were that comfortable, but walking instead of teetering proved more possible than she'd guessed. She could only hope the other stems in the shipment would be just as forgiving.

She was rummaging through the box, trying to decide which pair to try on next, when the entertainment segment of the twenty-four-hour news channel segued in. Her mouth fell open when she heard the name Reynolds Henry. She listened as the broadcaster repeated the headline.

The actor, who had faded into obscurity following a flash of fame and promise, had been found dead in his West Hollywood apartment of an apparent prescription-drug overdose. The broadcaster went on to present a brief montage chronicling Henry's troubled life.

Viva conjured an image of the lanky, blond actor whose biting wit and outspokenness had made him a fan favorite for a time. Her sympathies went out to him and the tragic path his life had taken. She knew that at one point or another, most actors' lives veered along similar stretches. More often than not, those stretches led to ends that mirrored Reynolds Henry's.

Viva had been among the thankful ones who'd managed to overcome the pitfalls and detours that could've made her life hell. Nevertheless, pitfalls and detours had not completely eluded her.

She'd made her own share of mistakes similar to the ones the TV broadcaster presented with such fervor in relation to Henry. She'd made those unfortunate decisions back in the early days, of her own accord. Though she'd certainly been well counseled on the dark situations and shady characters she'd encounter in the life she was seeking, she hadn't listened, hadn't wanted to and had feverishly rebelled against the truths her parents had dished her way. The truths Rook had dished her way…

What would he say if he knew of those mistakes? How would he react to seeing her unfortunate acts broadcasted on a TV screen? She wondered. How would he react were she to tell him?

Grimacing, Viva shook off the possibility. Did they have a chance? A new chance now in this recent turn of events? Did he miss her the way she missed him, or was his acceptance of Sophia's request to look out for her just him doing the right thing? Something that seemed to come so easily to him.

Was it as simple as all that? If not...then did she stand any chance at all of recapturing his heart—his love—if she revealed all to him? Hell, was that even necessary? It was the past—one she had no desire to revisit.

"Stop, V," she told herself, grimacing anew while tapping her nails to her temples. There was no need to torture herself. Best to leave things as they were.

Sophia's case would be closed soon enough. Murray would be dealt with one way or another and she'd be back to her life. Rook would carry on with his. And old truths? Old truths were best left where time had placed them. In the past.

It was foolish for her to even hope for anything fresh between her and Rook. She could accept that.

The bell sounded and she celebrated the intrusion while heading for the door. Seconds after pulling it open, all aspects of her pep talk fled from memory.

Rook stood in the hall.

Chapter 6

"Bad time?" Rook wanted to be the first to break the awkward silence.

"No," Viva said once she'd given herself an inward kick to hasten speech.

"You're sure?" He let his amber eyes drift down over her form-fitting black capri yoga pants to the chic high-heeled sandals that showcased her pedicure.

Viva followed the trail of his gaze and winced when discovery bloomed. "Leesi's going undercover," she said, citing the name of her on-screen character, Leesi Errol.

Rook grinned. "Looks like she's gonna be having a good time."

"The camera will make it look that way, but my feet are sure to be screaming the entire season."

"And yet you're using your free time to play around in them."

"Hardly." Viva waved Rook inside. "I gotta practice if I want to look authentic in these things."

Rook watched as she closed the door, approval no doubt lurking in his eyes. "I thought strolling around in those things would be like second nature to you."

"Well, I love heels." Viva gave the shoes a skeptical look. "*Stilts* are another matter altogether." She looked up in time to consider Rook's stare. "Is there a problem?"

"No problem at all." Rook's stare remained fixed.

Hoping for a change in subject, Viva motioned toward the TV. "Sounds like it's getting chillier out there. Can I get you some coffee? Sophia always makes way more than she can drink."

"Sounds good." Rook glanced over his shoulder. "Is she here?"

"She said she was heading to the precinct before going to her office. You could probably still catch her there if you came to see her."

"Actually, it's you I came to see."

Viva noticed the gold envelope he carried.

"Our boarding passes." He handed her the envelope. "I'm taking for granted that your passport's up to date?"

Viva laughed, accepting the packet. "That's an understatement. Yeah, I'm good there."

Rook nodded, his eyes resuming their provocative trek up her body. He could've easily emailed her the flight info, but was quite pleased with himself then for making the decision to come see her in person.

"Oh! The coffee." Viva hurried to the kitchen, teetering a bit on the towering heels. "Do you still take it with sugar and all that cream?"

"That's right." He followed her into the kitchen where he relaxed against the doorway to enjoy watching her move around.

Even in the heels, she still had trouble reaching the larger mugs on the uppermost shelf of the cabinet above the coffeemaker.

Pushing off the doorway, Rook went to help her at the cabinet. Cupping her hip, he urged her to still while he grabbed two mugs.

"Thanks," she said when he handed them to her. "I could've probably used more of this coffee last night instead of all the wine. I know I made a fool of myself. I just can't remember how *much* of a fool."

"That's funny," Rook said, maintaining his stance behind her. "I can't recall you making a fool of yourself either." Dipping his head, he inhaled the airy fragrance following her.

Viva turned then, searching his startling eyes with her own. "If you weren't a stronger man, you'd have woken up in my bed this morning."

"A stronger man…" He massaged the bridge of his nose as if suddenly weary. "A stronger man wouldn't have let you go in the first place." He stepped back, blinking as he suddenly noticed what he'd said. Additionally, he took note of how close he was to touching her—*really* touching her. Touching her the way he thought of whenever she crossed his mind, which was most days and every night.

With Olympian willpower, Rook stepped back. "I didn't come to interrupt you here, only to bring stuff for the trip."

"But—" Viva looked to the counter space "—your coffee."

"I shouldn't stay, V."

"Rook." She caught his wrist and squeezed. "If you insist on taking me with you to Italy, we're gonna be together most days, you know? No time like the present to see if we can handle—" She wasn't given the chance to finish the thought.

Rook had sudden possession of her mouth. The pressure was unforgiving, with a famished intensity, as if he were starving for her. Viva clung to him, her fingers half-curled into the fabric of his shirt. The height of the sandals put her just under his eye level and she could feel the breadth of his broad frame flush against her.

The kiss all but rendered Viva's hands useless, but not so for Rook. His roamed her body with all the familiarity of a skilled and patient lover. He cupped her generous bottom that was appealingly outlined in her snug pants. In the midst of squeezing, he lifted her until he was snug in the V of her thighs.

Viva couldn't deny the moan pressing for release inside her throat. With a subtle urgency to her moves, she worked herself nearer to him in search of heightened sensation.

Rook applied another decisive squeeze to Viva's bottom before he set her atop the counter. Viva's response was to link her shapely calves around his waist in order to keep him close.

She could feel him shifting into retreat mode and she wasn't ready to lose him yet, to lose him again...

Rook eased back, paying more attention to the drill-sergeant-like voice inside his head. The gruff voice warned against him being a slave to his hormones. Just the same, he teetered on the ragged edge of losing what ability he had to resist her when she loosed one of the sweet moans that stroked his ego like mink to the skin.

"V…" He meant for the murmur to evoke precaution. Instead, it held desire in a viselike grip.

Viva eased up from the counter to fuse herself against him. Her breasts crushed into his chest with every effort she made to breathe.

"V…" Rook reached deeper that time, seeking just an ounce of his evasive willpower. He swore he'd hold on to it for dear life once he found it. Hands firm on her waist, he set her back on the countertop and put his forehead to hers.

"I'd say we're even," he panted.

"Not—not really." Viva offered up a breathy laugh. "I at least had the decency to set my love scene in the bedroom."

Light laughter surged for Rook then too, but the gesture was brief. "I should go, V."

"I'm not asking you to."

"You should." He indulged in another whiff of the melon fragrance that clung to her skin and hair. "This isn't what we need."

"It is." She moved her brow against his cheek. "We need *this* and more." In spite of that, she decided to bite the bullet she'd dodged since the party. "We should also talk, Rook. *Really* talk."

"That's not a good idea."

The blunt refusal had her blinking in surprise and confusion.

"It's not a good idea for me." He put distance between them then.

Her confusion mounted, but it seemed Rook had exhausted his explanations.

"I'll be here a couple of hours before our flight leaves," he said and left her alone in the kitchen.

Elias Joss studied two of his four best friends in the world. His vivid blue-green stare was discerning in its steadiness.

"Did he say what this was about?" Eli asked.

"No," Linus said, and idly clinked salt and pepper shakers together, "but my guess is on Viva."

Elias nodded along with Tigo. The men had waited, at Rook's request, in a local bar and grill not far from the downtown headquarters of Joss Construction. The business had been established by Eli's father and was now jointly run between Eli, Santigo and Linus.

The guys didn't have long to wait. Rook arrived about ten minutes after their scheduled meeting time. Following handshakes, hugs, and the placing of food and drink orders, Rook got to the purpose of the gathering.

"She wants to talk," he said in a flat tone and watched his friends trade curious looks.

"Well…" Eli began a slow finger tap against the checkerboard tablecloth. "You know, um, that's a female thing. They…they like to talk. Come to think of it, it's a people thing…"

Laughter gained volume until it carried on a lively chord around the table.

Linus patted Rook's shoulder. "What's up, man? Talk to us."

Rook waited for the server to leave their drink orders. He appreciated the few additional moments to get his thoughts together. He needed them.

"I don't want to talk to her—not about what went wrong between us."

"What's changed, man?" Linus's concern was apparent.

"It's already too much. I can feel it."

At Rook's solemn admission, Tigo and Eli traded knowing looks.

"Are you sure you want us here, man?" Eli asked.

"I'm positive." Rook passed Eli a grateful smile. "I hoped seeing you guys—how happy you are…" He looked to Tigo and then shook his head while massaging the bunched muscles at his nape. "I thought it might change my mind about not wanting to fix things."

"Why wouldn't you want to fix things?" Linus asked.

"We're leaving, um…" Rook traded the neck massage for one that drove his thumb into the center of his palm. "I'm taking her with me on this trip. We'll be alone together for weeks."

"I see…and being together alone is so not the perfect time to talk and fix what's screwed up between you."

Linus's blatant sarcasm drew smiles from everyone, even Rook.

"We'll be alone," Rook reminded his friend once the laughter had eased.

"You wouldn't hurt her."

"I know that." Rook confirmed Linus's words without hesitation. "But talking about it…she'll see what it took me through and I…"

"You'll be stuck there," Eli guessed, "with no place to hide how she hurt you when she left."

"Exactly." Rook's grin was sly when it emerged. "Only she didn't leave—I did. She didn't want us to be over. She only wanted to go after what she'd been working for. It was me who all but said if she left we were done. *I* was the one who put that nail in our coffin."

"So tell her that," Tigo urged.

"And then what?" Rook countered, resting his hands palms up on the big, sturdy table. "Watch her go back to her life when all this is done?"

"She might not want that," Linus said.

Rook's grin meshed with laughter. "I'm about to relocate out of the country, remember? She's just reconnecting with her family. How's all this supposed to work?"

"You're grabbing at excuses," Eli warned.

"You're right." Rook took a moment to mop his face with his palms. "If I tell V all this and I still don't get her back…" He looked to Linus. "It'll be worse than before. I don't want to think about what happens if I can't come back from it. She's already blaming herself—I could see it in her eyes when she said she wanted to talk." He sipped the locally brewed beer he'd ordered.

"Us talking," he continued, "me coming clean about what I went through, what anger did to me… she'll think it was her fault no matter how much I tell her it wasn't."

"So don't take her with you," Tigo blurted. "Between all of us and that warrior squad you've got at L Sec, we can keep her safe until Soap's case is closed and she's out of the woods." He reached across the table, squeezed Rook's wrist. "Go talk to her, spill all this and give her time to deal with it around here with her folks. You go handle your business in Italy. Get all this old drama off your chest and go find out what it feels like to live out from under the weight of it."

Shrugging, Tigo reached for his beer mug and raised it in toast. "Come back here with a new perspective. At the very least, you'll have slayed a demon that's been riding your back for way too long."

There was silence following Tigo's words. After a moment, Eli clapped a hand to his friend's back.

"I swear he's gotten smarter since he's gotten Sophia back by his side where she belongs," Eli teased and joined in when laughter followed.

"Sounds like a damn good plan to me," Linus added.

"It does." Relaxing back in his chair, Rook fixed his friends with an easy smile.

"We could've waited another day or two to do this, you know? You and Rook aren't leaving until—"

"No, Soap, I needed to get this out while I still had my nerve." Viva added a shaky laugh. "Thanks for letting me be involved in this."

"I know it's got to be hard talking about such sticky stuff regarding someone who gave you your big break," Sophia said as she squeezed her sister's arm.

Viva nodded. "Whatever Murray's into needs to come to an end. It's probably weird, but in a way, maybe I'm helping him." She snorted a laugh.

Sophia joined in. "Sounds perfectly sane to me."

Viva sent her sister a skeptical look. "You sure you

want to be using the term 'perfectly sane' and my name in the same sentence?"

"I think we're safe." Sophia left the conference table in her office to top off her coffee and get more hot water for Viva's tea. "You think you'll hear from Murray again?" she asked.

"Not sure." Viva blew at a coiled lock dangling across her brow. "He sounded pretty resolved when we talked."

"I see." Sophia prepped her coffee and added hot water to a new mug for Viva. "Guess that'll leave lots of time for you and Rook to talk, huh?"

"I'm not so sure," Viva said once she'd considered her sister's words for a while. "He came over this morning."

"Well, well…" Playful intrigue sharpened Sophia's features when she turned from the counter with mugs in hand. "You guys pick up from where you left off the night before?"

Viva tried to deny it but couldn't, especially when she betrayed just the faintest flush beneath the light caramel tone of her skin.

Sophia laughed, no doubt noticing her sister's color darken. "I'll take that as a yes."

"Not a *full* yes," Viva argued.

"Now *that* sounds weird." Sophia set down the mugs.

"He pulled away. I mean… I know one of us needed to and I—I certainly wasn't trying—" Viva shook her head, having spied the delight in Sophia's expression. "I told him we needed to talk and he—he said it wasn't a good idea. It wasn't a good idea for him."

"Hmm…more weirdness. Maybe the timing was bad?"

Viva left the table where they'd recorded her statement that afternoon. "I don't think that was it. It sounded more personal than the timing being bad because he was running late for an appointment."

"Will you try talking to him again? Maybe once you guys are in Italy?" Sophia sipped her coffee and watched her sister consider the questions.

"This is something I should tell him before Italy, I think."

"And it's something you don't expect him to take too well."

"I *know* he won't take it too well."

"Just tell him, V." Sophia came around to the side of the table where Viva stood. "Don't worry about whether he thinks it's a good idea or not. Don't even act like you're about to get into it. Just spill it and let the chips fall."

"Yeah." Viva worried her bottom lip between her thumb and forefinger. "That's just what I had in mind, only what he said about talking not being a good idea for him—it unsettled me, Soap."

Concern on her face, Sophia set her mug onto the table. "How?"

"How's he been, Sophia?" Viva fixed her sister with a stern stare. "How's he *really* been?"

"He's been *really* busy and gotten *really* successful."

Viva's resulting laughter was genuine as it bubbled up. "That's good."

"L Sec's been involved with all kinds of big-name clients from all over the world. Much of that happened when Rook added the training end for his clients who wanted their own in-house personnel trained. That got the attention of the sports and entertainment industries—athletes wanting to diversify their workouts, studio types seeing the same for the stunt teams they hired."

"I'm glad for him, Sophia." Viva walked away from the table, picked up her tea on the way past. "But how's *he* been? Beyond all the success of the business, I mean?"

"Honey…" Sophia winced as though she were reluctant to share. "We've gone over this before… You—you know he hasn't been a hermit. No man who looks the way he does would go for long without being noticed by at least fifty women, nor would he shun their advances for long. No matter how in love he is with one of Hollywood's most lusted-after women."

"Well, damn! Did you just compliment me?" Viva faked amazement.

Sophia gave a casual shrug, reached for her coffee. "It's hard, but I'm trying to make an effort."

"Understood." Viva laughed. "But what I'm asking is if you think he's changed. He was always the easygoing sort—laid-back, hard to rile."

"You want to know if your leaving tapped into his temper." Sophia gave an understanding nod. "V, I'd bet my badge that nothing you could tell him would ever break him down so far that he'd put his hands on you that way."

"God, Sophia…" Viva moaned. "That's one of the few things I'm certain of. It's not *me* I'm worried about."

Sophia's expression then was one of renewed realization. "What you have to tell him involves Murray, doesn't it?"

"Not totally." Viva sighed, launched a more determined pace around the office. "But he brushes up against it. I don't want whatever I say to have him lashing out in a way that could hurt him. He doesn't need that—not because of Murray or anyone else I'm connected to. It's not worth it."

"This sounds serious, V." Sophia's face tightened with signs of rigid concern. "Sure it's not something you'd care to share with your baby sis?"

"Hell, Soap, *I* barely want to think about it. Talking it over with my kid sister, my family at all, isn't something I can do without feeling sick inside."

"So why tell Rook?"

"Because my leaving wasn't his fault." Viva pivoted on the chic but sensible peach-colored pumps that accentuated the sharp cuff of the cream trousers she wore. "My leaving would've happened whether or not our relationship had been reduced to us behaving like passing ships. Fact is, things being strained between us made it all easier for me. I left and quickly discovered Rook was so right about the people I left with."

"Listen, V, not to brag, but I do wield a certain amount of power." Sophia set her long legs apart in an intentionally confrontational stance. "Say the word and I'll move mountains to have them arrested."

Viva laughed amid her distress, loving her little sister very much and appreciating her support. "It's not necessary, hon, but thanks."

"But you think Rook would want to kill someone over it?"

"I know he would." Viva hurriedly closed the distance between her and Sophia, grasped Sophia's hands and squeezed out of a sudden need for reassurance. "I know Rook would never hurt me, but he'll damn well hate me once I tell him."

Following the lunch with his friends, Rook decided to put in a quick call to Viva and see if she was free to talk. There was no time like the present, he'd decided, yet his fingers faltered over the screen when he scrolled through his contacts for her number.

Best not to rouse any preconceived notions on her part with a phone call. Best to bite this particular nail right through its rusted head. Rook was tossing the phone to the passenger seat and slipping behind the wheel of the Suburban when the screen lit up with an incoming call. He toyed with not answering, until he glimpsed Burt Larkin's name. He took the call before it transitioned to voice mail.

"Interrupting anything?" Burt queried once the connection was made.

"No, I'm headed back to the office."

"Have you seen Viva today?"

"This morning and, word to the wise, she's gonna start ducking you if you ask for any more autographs."

"Yeah." Burt tried for lightness with the response, but the effort fell flat. "This isn't about that, Rook."

"Tell me." Rook's suspicion niggled its way through fast and deep.

"Has she mentioned a Reynolds Henry?"

"No. Why?"

"He was a client of Murray Dean's and he's dead."

Chapter 7

The talk with Sophia had helped. Viva hadn't realized how much she'd needed to vent about the situation with Rook. It was a situation that, until her return
home, had resided very amicably in the recesses of her
mind where other events of the past went to languish.

Still, the fact that she very much wanted to have
the discussion with Rook was an issue that not even
a hearty chat with her sister could extinguish. Yet,
Sophia's question had replayed in her head on a loop
since she'd left city hall to return to Sophia's condo.

So why tell Rook?

Yes, he deserved to know that she'd gone off half-
cocked and made a mistake that solidified the doom
of their relationship. Couldn't she just tell him that and
leave out all the ugly details? If only…

Viva rushed into the lobby and sent a quick smile to

the desk guards on her way past. Quickly, she doffed the elements of her disguise and was shoving shades and a scarf into her tote. The elevator doors opened and before she could take a step forward, she was escorted none too gently inside.

"Hey—" She caught herself, realizing it was Rook who held her. "Didn't think I'd see you again today."

"Plans have changed." He kept hold of her arm even after the door slid closed with a soothing bump. "Are you packed?"

Viva turned as much as his hold would allow. There was no need to study his face, it was an unreadable mask. "I, um, sure. I haven't been in town long enough to fully unpack so… Rook? What's going on?"

"We leave for Italy in the morning."

She tried to face him more fully then. "Why? What's changed?"

There was no answer from her escort and Viva allowed that scene to play out until they were inside her sister's condo.

"Look, don't get me wrong. I actually find the stony silence sexy." She tossed the tote bag to the sofa and watched him prowl the living room on a security check. "You're still gonna have to come up with some info if you expect me to fly halfway around the world with you tomorrow."

She spread her hands in a silent question that went unanswered when he moved on through the condo, completing his check. "My guess is I won't have time to see my family again before we leave." She folded her arms over the silky peach cargo blouse and tried to match his stony look with her own when he returned to the living room.

His response was not what she'd expected.

"Do you know a Reynolds Henry?"

"Reynolds?" She shed some of her stony veneer. "Well, yeah, I, um, he's an actor. He hasn't worked in a while." She cast a sidelong glance to the flat screen across the room. "If the news I heard this morning is true, he won't have the chance to change that. They say he's dead."

"They were right." Rook's closed expression adopted a grim quality that lent a fiercer element to his caramel-doused features. "Did you know he was a client of Murray's?"

Viva opened her mouth, but no response emerged. Shaky then on her pumps, she settled on to the arm of the nearest chair. "He was… I'd forgotten." The ebony flecks danced in her eyes when she suddenly looked to Rook. "The news reported it was a suicide."

Rook's smile did nothing to diminish his grim expression. "You've been in the business long enough to know how often stories are spun."

"Yeah." Viva studied the carpet without really seeing it. Those words were especially true when the story involved political and entertainment figures. She fixed Rook with a hopeful look. "Do you know what really happened?"

"News said he overdosed on prescription meds, which is true, but word from the lead investigators is that every pill he had was laced with four times the prescribed amount. He would've been dead whether or not he'd taken his meds as instructed."

"But how could you know that already?" Viva pushed off the chair arm. "Even I know it takes longer than a day to get back a tox report." Rook's bland look had her stiffening.

There was a reason his security firm was one of the most sought-after entities worldwide, she reminded herself. Obtaining preliminary details on matters such as these was perhaps among the more unremarkable feats his organization was capable of.

"What are you thinking?" she asked.

"I think you know."

"I don't believe I do." Yet, she stiffened anew when he merely stared. "You can't be thinking Murray would…" She couldn't finish the notion. "Why?" she asked instead.

"What was it he said during your conversation about putting things to bed?"

"By killing his clients? What sense would that make?"

"Oh, I don't know, V. In case they'd seen things that could be hard for him or his more elusive associates to explain away? Who knows?" He stalked the living room, his amber stare seeming more radiant in the wake of agitation. "These clients might take a chance on going to the cops and sharing things that have them concerned, especially if one of them's got a sister on the force."

"Me?" Viva plastered both hands to her chest. "Seriously, Rook? You honestly think he'd come after me that way?" She sounded incredulous, but couldn't ignore the dip her heart took to her stomach.

"Even with all you know and have seen, you still can't bring yourself to believe the worst about the man." Rook shook his head, frustration fixed indelibly on his face.

"That's not it."

"Then what is it?"

"Rook, I—Murray, he—he's got a lot of questionable... He's not... He—"

"Save it." Rook glanced around the living room once more and then sized Viva up with one heated sweep of his stare. "I'll be back in the morning. Use the time to finish packing. I'll make sure you have time to see your folks before the flight. Don't try calling Murray again."

"And if he calls me?" She watched him bow his head and grin a grin that was more malicious than humor filled.

"I know it's hard for you to take my advice seriously when it comes to Murray," he began, "but maybe you could try giving it just a shred of consideration in this case."

He left her then and Viva remained where she stood long after he'd gone.

Belluno, Italy

Rook and Viva arrived in Northern Italy close to 2:00 in the morning. The town of Belluno was a province in the Veneto region. Rook had fallen in love with the neighboring Cortina d'Ampezzo and had decided to own a home there regardless of how his business played out.

As his primary business would be handled in Belluno, the plan was to spend the night at a hotel in town. Rook had arranged to meet with his associates a little earlier than planned, given the change in the arrival date to Italy. Afterward, he and Viva were scheduled to leave for Cortina.

The departure from Philadelphia had been a prompt, teary one filled with goodbyes and light on details. Sophia had, at least, received more insight on the reasons for the change. Viva had sat nearby while Rook shared his findings on Reynolds Henry's passing and how he factored Murray Dean into it all. Viva wasn't surprised that her sister all but carried her to the airport and buckled her into the seat. Rook received the chief of Ds' full blessings to head out of the States with quickness.

Viva didn't mind. Italy was a dreamland in spite of its frigid temps and the generally rainy, snowy and windy climate of the area during that time of year. The environment wasn't such a jolt given the already dipping temps back in the States. Viva found it to be heavenly.

Or...it could've been were it not for Rook's mood, which was proving to rival the region's atmosphere for chilliness. What had triggered his attitude was no surprise nor was it a reaction she could argue. He had every right to be pissed, especially when the topic of their current unrest was the very last thing they'd argued over and what had signaled the demise of their relationship. Viva knew and understood Rook's feelings toward Murray. What she couldn't understand was how he could so easily believe the agent could be capable of murder.

She inhaled the crisp air that swept in from the Schiara mountain range of the Dolomites. Reluctantly, she risked a quick scan of the tarmac in search of Rook. She found him among a circle of suited men, enjoying what appeared to be a rather jovial conversation. With clear, cold air filtering her mind, her voice of reason began to elevate and echo.

If Murray was capable of involving himself in the kinds of things she'd shared with the police less than twenty-four hours earlier, why wouldn't he be capable of murder? Reminding herself that she wasn't dead yet was a weak and hardly reassuring fact.

Could he really be that paranoid? She wondered and found herself replaying the conversation with his assistant. Artesia Relis had believed her boss to be "riled up" enough to contact her. The woman had surely held her job for long enough to handle the infrequent uprisings of a Hollywood agent. Even still, Arty was more than a little agitated over the pressures of her job. She'd sounded downright worried.

Then there was her own conversation with Murray and his assurances that all would be well once he'd put certain things to bed. If she was among them, would he have been so bold as to tell her? Perhaps Reynolds was involved in those aspects of Murray's allegedly illegal dealings. Viva was sure Sophia was at work investigating that very angle.

She shook her head then, realizing she was filling it with too much angst. Much more of that and both her sister and her ex would be agreeing on putting her in an asylum instead of the wonderland beauty of Northern Italy.

With that thought in mind, not to mention the fact that she was lending too much time to worry and not enough to opportunity, Viva got herself in check. After all, Rook's new home was also the place where shopping dreams were made.

Cortina was home to the most drooled-over names in haute couture—Gucci, Bulgari, Benetton. Oh yes, it was a shopper's paradise and she intended to take thorough advantage.

When she felt warm hands on her arms Viva's thoughts pivoted back to Rook. Even through the bulky fabric of her wool peacoat, she recognized his touch. She savored the feel of him as his hands moved up and down her arms.

"You're going to catch your death out here."

Smiling, Viva enjoyed the breadth of his magnificent chest when he pulled her back against it.

"I opt for catching it out here," she sighed. "I like that better than the other places currently vying for the title."

Rook's hands stilled until he was turning Viva to face him. A fierce glint lurked in his dazzling stare then. "Don't you think that," he commanded while giving her a slight shake in the process.

It was hard for Viva to obey. "Why shouldn't I? You believe my own agent might try to kill me."

"Jesus, V." Rook closed his eyes and hung his head for a second or three. "I shouldn't have put that in your head."

"It's not such a far stretch," she said, hearing misery claim her voice. "Makes perfect sense given where things stand."

"I still shouldn't have said it. There are lots of other explanations just as valid. It's just that I can't afford to take any chances."

"But you still believe he's capable of taking a life?" she challenged. "You think he may've taken Reynolds's?"

"I shouldn't have said that either. It was anger talking."

Viva gave a smile that was just as miserable as her former expression. "It's okay to be angry."

"It's not okay for me."

"Signor Lourdess? Are you and the signorina ready?"

The driver's inquiry interrupted Viva's mounting curiosity and her intentions to question Rook's haunted admission.

"Thanks, Luca." Rook sent the man a quick nod and smile before his hands tightened at Viva's arms. Then he was leading her to the waiting limo and getting her settled in the back of the sleek gray vehicle.

"You may want to get out of that coat," he suggested once Luca had shut the car door, securing them inside. "It's over fifteen minutes to the hotel." He looked out the window at the white sky. "We'll probably wake up to snow by morning."

"Thought I saw a few flakes while I waited for you to finish up."

Faint concern dwelled in his eyes. "You should've gotten into the car."

"I didn't mind and it was nice seeing you get acquainted with your new business associates."

Rook raised a brow. "They aren't my associates yet."

"So they're still trying to decide if you can give them what they want?" Viva slipped out of the rich tan-colored wool.

"Oh, they already know that I can," Rook remarked without an ounce of arrogance, only unshakable confidence. "This trip is about whether *I'm* willing to pull up stakes in order to give it to them."

Viva laughed. "Ahh...so *you're* being wooed, huh?"

"Seems so." Rook tossed his brown leather jacket to the long seat opposite the one he and Viva shared.

"And how do your guys feel about that?" She listened as Rook shared his plans.

The executive team would interchange relocation—six months in Italy, six months in the States. Rook explained that the goal was to interview local candidates who would oversee day-to-day operations in the future. Any member of the executive team would be welcome to live there abroad or head back to the States.

"None of them have personal ties that'd prevent them from making the leap if they decided to," he finished.

"So they're loners just like their boss?" Laughter mingled with Viva's words. She watched him smooth a hand across his head, a move her eyes followed with longing. She wished it were her fingers gliding across the close crop of waves.

"They're not like their boss." Rook smirked, appearing quietly amused. "At least they've got *some* semblance of a social life."

"Are you saying you live like a hermit?"

"For the most part, I guess," he admitted, following a moment's consideration. "I suppose that's best."

Shaking her head, Viva tucked her legs up on the car seat. "I'm sure every woman in Philadelphia would disagree with you on that." The interior lighting was a low golden gleam, but enough illumination for her to study him closely then, glimpsing a reaction she'd classify as a cross between regret and resolve. The muscle flexing along his jaw was one she recognized all too well as a signal that his frustration was mounting.

The very last thing she wanted was for either of them to be experiencing frustration there. Sadly, she didn't hold out much hope of them having much chance at avoiding it. At any rate, she hoped they could at least try for one night without it.

With a sigh, Viva uncurled her legs to unzip the chic block-heeled boots she'd worn for the trip. She wriggled her toes indulgently once she tugged off the shoes and tossed them to the opposite side of the dim cabin. She heard Rook's chuckle, a second before she caught his animated expression. "What?" A half smile curved her mouth.

"I see your shoes are still one of the first things you come out of?"

Viva slid an amused look toward the abandoned boots and shrugged. "Ten minutes barefoot sounds like heaven to me."

"Hmph, sounds like you're about to have your work cut out for you." At her confusion, Rook explained, "Getting used to those neck breakers you brought along for the show."

Viva waved off his concern and settled back against the decadent suede cushioning of the seat. "I'm not worried. The camera will mask the majority of my discomfort." She laughed softly. "You'd be surprised by how big an ally the camera can be when you develop a love affair with it. Still…" She gave another indulgent wiggle of her toes. "They're finicky, so you have to know how to sweet-talk them."

Rook's expression was fixed. His stirring gaze appeared even more brilliant given the intensity with which he watched her then. "I don't think you'd have to do much sweet talking. The camera's a slave to what it sees after all."

The unexpected compliment sent arousal plumbing her core with shocking ruthlessness. At any rate, Viva was in no mood to make her needs known only to have him deny her. Instead, she turned, intending to seek solace at the other end of the long, wide seat.

She found herself on her back instead, with Rook's chest against hers. The throbbing at her core became a relentless vibration that seemed to take command of her entire body. Her fingers sank into the luxurious fleece of his midnight-blue sweatshirt in an effort to draw him closer as well as to cease the mad tremble of her fingers.

The effort was basically useless. Sensation had her all but begging him to give her what had been ravaging her dreams for far too long.

Rook's thoughts, however, seemed to be traveling along the same vein as the woman he held. He found the fastening of her dress, releasing it with a dexterous touch. The zipper tab followed from its hiding place snug beneath her arm on the curve-hugging frock.

The move told Viva that he'd most likely scoped out the tab's inconspicuous location the moment she'd arrived in her sister's living room dressed for the trip.

The zipper made barely a sound as he tugged the tab to its lowest point. The material gaped open at Viva's side, providing easy access to her breasts heaving against the lacy, black cups of her bra.

Viva bit her lip to still its quivering, when spasms rocked her as Rook's wide palm covered one of the lace-covered mounds and squeezed. The move was followed by the moan-inducing trip his thumb made around one straining nipple. She wanted so much more than what he was giving her.

Grudgingly, Viva acknowledged that dressing for the weather, not to mention their current location, was going to make a lustier exploration impossible. She treated herself by delighting in the sheer pleasure of having him so near. Rook didn't crush her beneath him, but gave her enough of his considerable weight to bring an approving smile to her mouth.

Viva found her way beneath his sweatshirt. She pouted for a moment when her nails encountered another shirt beneath instead of the taut skin she sought. The shirt hung outside loose-fitting corduroys and she made quick work of fumbling beneath the hem, only to discover a T-shirt tucked neatly inside the waistband.

Hissing a curse, she slammed a fist to his side. "What's with all these clothes?" she grumbled.

"It's cold outside." His reminder was muffled where his mouth was busy at the base of her throat.

"Maybe I should've worn more under my dress," she huffed, "even though my efforts don't seem to be appreciated—"

Her words were smothered by a kiss that sent moans filling the cabin. Viva heard her own voice as well as Rook's. Knowing the moment was to be completely savored, she threaded her fingers through the short, sleek curls of his hair. She smiled, even as her mouth was ravaged by the driving plunges of his tongue.

She had almost—*almost*—forgotten how luxurious his hair was, how taut and unyielding his body was, how sweetly overpowering he felt against her. Viva tried to drive her tongue against his using the same potent thrusts, but she was no match, not against the hunger that fueled his kiss.

He seemed okay with her not being able to do much more than take what he gave her, so Viva didn't see much need to change the status quo. Her strokes in his hair took on a less frantic display. She was roasting inside the dress, despite the fact that he'd already unzipped it. She may have bit her tongue to resist begging him to do more. Happily, her tongue was already engaged in an act she dared not interrupt.

Once Rook had ventured beneath the already hiked hem of her dress, Viva was positively purring beneath him. When he broke the kiss, she gulped in much-needed air and at the same time cursed him for breaking their contact.

"And you talk to *me* about too many clothes?" His voice sounded like a low rumble, yet it was easily decipherable in the quiet confines of the car.

Viva felt his hands at her hips, cradling her bottom encased in a pair of thick tights.

"You only need to tug," she said in a breathy tone that had somewhat become her celebrity calling card, and bumped her hips to his for emphasis.

Rook didn't require the nudge as he was already easing down the tights. He could have cursed the fever that drove him like an inexperienced teen, but just then he was welcoming it. The zeal rushed his veins like some form of adrenaline to which there was no comparison.

He hadn't denied himself a woman's touch since losing Viva. Instead, he'd indulged—overmuch at times. He'd been determined to scour her from the walls of his memory. Those romps had done the trick momentarily. He'd been able to lose himself in lust. But only because he'd refused to acknowledge that the sensation fell far short of what he'd known with Viva.

Rook nuzzled his face deep into the fragrant hollow at Viva's neck, groaning as his palms filled with her derriere. Though the mounds were toned, they maintained the feminine lushness that stiffened his sex, which was straining almost painfully against his button fly.

The low growl of a curse had Viva surfacing from the haze of her arousal. She knew Rook's reaction wasn't in response to the sensuality they were losing themselves in. Thankfully, he didn't give her long to wonder at the sudden change in his mood.

"We're turning off the main road. We'll be at the hotel soon," he said.

Viva didn't bother asking if they had to stop. That answer, though disappointing, was obvious. What wasn't obvious and what she most wanted an answer to, was whether they could finish what they'd started.

Chapter 8

With the exception of the front desk and maintenance staff, the Hotel Oasi was awash in silence when Rook and Viva arrived. The snowfall that had begun at the airport had continued to drift steadily and was dusting the hotel's picturesque grounds by the time they'd exited the car.

In spite of the quiet beauty, Viva felt as though she had a twenty-piece brass section performing inside her head. Sexual frustration had been an aspect of her life that she'd learned to live with. She hadn't exactly lived like a hermit, but she hadn't been the free spirit the media often tried to label members of her world.

There had been a brief…thing between her and her leading man, which had been more to generate buzz for their show than true love. While she and Bryce Danzig were good friends, which made them a provocative on-screen duo, there had been nothing more.

Still, she had made the effort at a real life outside the Hollywood hustle. Sadly, it was the Hollywood hustle that had made sustaining or even acquiring a real relationship impossible or hardly worth the effort.

The seamless check-in process consisted of Rook's signature on a pad. Then, they made their way to the elevator bay to embark upon a smooth ascent in a glass car lit by recessed gold lighting. As her heels sank into thick chocolate carpeting, Viva realized how wiped she was. The mellow environment allowed that fact to seep in. She gave a pronounced blink and fought to keep her eyes open. When she muffled a yawn behind a gloved hand, Rook pulled her into the reassuring shelter of his embrace. Viva shut her eyes and allowed the steady beat of his heart to lead her into escape.

The elevator bumped to a gentle stop and the baggage handler escorted them down another expansive corridor. Rook kept a supportive arm about Viva's waist and she couldn't help but think how that simple touch was more secure than any of the elaborate measures her status deemed her worthy of.

The handler disengaged the locks and double doors opened into a sumptuous suite lit by a single clay-based lamp in a far corner of the palatial living room. Heavy burgundy drapes were parted to reveal the snow falling across the hotel grounds.

Viva took in the beauty of the suite while Rook tipped the handler once the man had returned from placing the luggage in the designated rooms. She continued her tour, approval curving her lips when her hands sank into the back of a plush sofa she passed.

Rich auburn suede gave beneath a mound of softness she envisioned herself sinking into. For the second time that evening, she unzipped her boots and decided there was no time like the present. She sank into the suede sofa, comfort wrapping her in an embrace.

Rook had seen off the handler and was then occupied by his phone when it chimed with a notification. Viva remembered she'd not taken her mobile off airplane mode since they'd landed, so she decided to check her missed calls, as well.

Comfort and serenity fled once the screen activated before her eyes.

Opening his phone to more than ten missed calls was nothing new to Rook. He hadn't as yet, he thought with much relish, developed an emotional attachment to the device. He saw the text from Burt who had also made the ten missed calls. There was a link to a breaking news story. Upon scanning it, Rook's eyes shifted to Viva.

He'd noticed she'd settled onto one of the room's lengthy sofas and was pleased that she might actually get some rest while they were away. Though her clothes and makeup were perfect despite the nine-hour flight, he could still detect the traces of exhaustion in her warm stare. He saw her sit up on the sofa and then stand with the phone clutched in her shaking hand.

"There's nothing you can do for her, V."

Viva turned to Rook as if she were dazed. Her expression revealed that she hadn't wholly deciphered his words to her. She blinked rapidly several times before her eyes tracked to his phone and understanding wedged in alongside devastation.

"I could be there." Her voice was small but determined.

"And be among what, V? Seventy other people already crowding into her hospital room?"

Viva considered his phone with a measuring look. "I only have the info the doctors gave my cast mates. I'm guessing you've got more."

Rook knew that to encourage her to let the subject alone was a waste of his time. He didn't try. Instead, he opened Burt's text. "This'll be breaking within the hour, I'm told. Bevy Ward?" He looked to Viva for confirmation on the name and watched her move from the sofa as she nodded.

"She plays my sister on the show."

Rook nodded as he got a mental image of the actress who played Pamela Errol on the hit show. "She'd just taken the exit off the expressway leading to her place in the Hollywood Hills."

"She must've had a late night out that way," Viva muttered, biting her thumbnail as she paced the area between the sofa and coffee table. "She hates that place."

"Her car hit a guardrail, spun out…" Rook trailed off at the look Viva sent his way. He let an agitated curse die a quick death on his tongue and continued with the story.

"The rest of this hasn't been released to the press. Prelim reports from authorities on scene say marks on the driver's side *could be* consistent with it being sideswiped by another vehicle. There were no other vehicles in the vicinity when Ms. Ward was found. She's got no family, so an attempt was made to contact her agent, Murray Dean. He couldn't be reached. Ms. Ward's costars from her show were then contacted."

Viva let out a whoosh of breath and lost her interest in pacing. She settled back onto the sofa but the cushiony furnishing did little to soothe her that time.

"The reports are preliminary, V," Rook said, in a soft reminder. Silently, he held to the idea that they were more than accurate.

Viva apparently subscribed to that same theory. "Someone ran her off the road, didn't they?"

"I don't need you worrying over this, V—"

"Someone ran her off the road. Bevy is a client of Murray's. Surely you aren't going to try to convince me that this is all one big coincidence?"

"No." Rook set aside his phone. "I won't try to convince you of that."

"I need to be there, Rook." Viva made a shaky attempt to stand.

"Viva—"

"Bev's not just my sister on TV, Rook. There's real closeness there." Emotion fired hotly in Viva's eyes. "You may think that's a bunch of shallow bull, but it's true." She paused, willing back the tears. "When things were at their lowest between me and my family, it was Bev who kept me from going off the deep end."

Smiling reflectively, Viva resumed her slow pacing. She hugged herself as she moved. "She'd always say she was an only child and would've liked to experience some of that sibling angst. 'Only *some*, V,' she'd say… 'I don't think I could handle it three hundred and sixty-five days a year.'" The laughter left Viva's voice and was replaced then by a pleading tone that matched the look she sent to Rook.

"I need to be there."

Rook held firm. "I'm sorry, V."

The pleading look cooled and her gaze went flat.

"Don't let all the permissions my sister's granted you go to your head. I'm only putting up with this 'hiding out' nonsense to make Sophia happy."

"Maybe you should've considered what that would mean before you agreed to it."

Viva burst into quick, harsh laughter. "Like I had any choice!"

"Are you trying to say I bullied you?"

She tilted her head and sneered. "Do you really need to hear me tell you that you did?"

He shrugged. "It's news to me. You never struck me as a woman who reacted well to being bullied. Had I known differently, I may've tried it years ago."

"I know what you're up to." Viva massaged an ache forming near her temples. "This side argument isn't going to make me forget about wanting to go be with my friend."

"Even if it means putting your own life on the line to get there?"

Viva steeled herself against reiterating the fact that Murray wouldn't hurt her—not now. Not when Bev was— God…had he really been responsible for that? She looked to Rook again.

"Does your information say what her condition is?"

Rook's mouth tightened, and he didn't look too eager to share. "She's in bad shape," he confirmed finally. "Broken leg, fractured collarbone. There was some internal bleeding, but they've been able to stop that."

Viva turned her back to Rook when the news reached her ears. She could feel the pressure of tears returning with a vicious intensity. She despised the feel of tears, despised even more anyone seeing her give in to them. Correction—she despised Rook Lourdess seeing her give in to them.

He moved closer, halted within a few inches of touching distance. "You'll know anything I do, the moment I do."

She turned back to him. "And then what?"

"And then you'll know." Rook told himself to let her go when she elbowed past him to leave the room. "V?" he called anyway.

She stopped, but didn't turn to face him.

"Your room's behind the double doors to your left."

Some of the rigidness left Viva's shoulders as despair claimed her. They'd both been of one accord when they'd stepped into the suite. They'd thought of nothing but finishing what they'd started in the car. Now, one more element of unrest between them made that possibility seem more like fantasy.

"Good night, Rook."

He winced at the finality of the statement. Regardless of how unfortunate the evening had turned out, he knew it was best to set out the rest of the ugly cards before they parted ways.

"I know a trip to Italy or anywhere else in the world for you is like going to the post office for others." He smiled grimly when she remained where she was, her back still turned to him. "You can find your way back from here to LA with your eyes closed," he continued.

"I hope you won't do that, but to cut down on the confusion, I thought I'd go on and take this."

Viva turned then, the renewed exhaustion in her eyes making way for a sudden storm to brew as she fixed on what he held—her passport.

"You horse's ass," she spat, bristling when the delicious roughness of his laughter vibrated in the room. She'd heard enough of the gesture to know he was genuinely amused.

"I know you can swear better than that, V. I have the chance to hear it every Saturday night between the hours of ten and eleven."

"Wow." Her smile was chilly. "I'd expect you to be up to more than sitting in front of the TV on a Saturday night."

He responded with a playful roll of his stunning eyes and a lopsided grin. "A man can do a lot in front of a TV. It all depends on what he's watching."

She noticed the glint in his gaze and knew he was teasing her ruthlessly. Realizing that stung. Between the two of them, she was clearly the only one who gave in to pleasuring herself to the memory of their sex life.

Images emerged as those memories surfaced and she was suddenly sweltering inside the already warm dress. She considered him with a look as suspicious as it was measuring.

"I guess you really don't trust me, do you? I gave my word to Sophia, you know?"

"To Sophia—not to me."

"I thought that was understood."

"So did I—once."

She gave an amused snort. "You were right. I didn't think this through before I gave my word. It was so *not* a good idea."

"Well, it's done." He slipped the passport book into a back pocket. "You're stuck with me, so we better make the most of it."

"There was a time when that would've been all I wanted."

He wouldn't let her remark rile him—*couldn't* let it rile him. "A time, huh? When was that? While you were planning your great escape?"

"Like you noticed!" Viva had no problem releasing the tethers on her own temper. "You didn't have a clue until I was practically waving my plane ticket under your nose!" She watched his remarkable gaze flare before he closed his eyes with a slow flutter of unfairly long lashes and bowed his head. It was another move she'd seen often enough—usually when he was stressed over some business matter. Now, she knew the reaction was all for her. Some perverse part of her welcomed the coming explosion.

Such was not to be. Viva watched, fascinated by the way he tamped down the anger as suddenly as it had risen. It was as if he'd made a silent decision against saying anything more. She laughed, unamused when he began to leave the room.

"So even here, even now, we aren't going to discuss this?"

"We aren't going to discuss this," he replied as he stopped and looked at her, "especially not here."

"I'm not afraid of you, Rook." The tiniest sliver of her apprehension eased when his laughter mounted—the one signifying honest amusement.

"I know you're not afraid of me, V. I'm a damn good teacher and I taught you how to defend yourself."

That sweltering feeling returned to place a fiery layer over those memories. Those lessons hadn't been sensual in nature, yet they'd led to events that were of the most carnal variety. She couldn't control her memories and knew by his emerging smile that he could tell his words had taken her thoughts down the route he'd intended.

Viva managed a quiet clearing of her throat and hoped that her voice would cooperate. "I meant I'm not afraid of anything you might say. Chances are high I've probably said the same thing to myself a million times. Rook, we need to put this to rest once and for all, regardless of where it leads...or doesn't lead."

"*You're* not afraid of what I might say, but I am." He swept her with a probing, potent stare. "We aren't getting into this now, V." *Just wait until we're back home*, he silently begged her. *I'll tell you everything you* think *you want to hear.* He knew the only place it would go would be back to the lives they'd led for the past six years.

Viva knew more conversation on the subject would prove useless, but she couldn't resist one last jab. "Once again, it's about what *you* want."

"Guess it's about time I know what that feels like." His smile was a chilly slash across his face and he resumed the trek to his room.

"Don't try making any clever travel arrangements with your phone either. I wouldn't mind having it to keep your passport company," he called over a shoulder.

Viva stood steaming inside her dress and stewing in anger as she watched him stroll from view.

Plain stubbornness kept Viva from venturing outside her room to hunt down breakfast the next morning. By some miracle, she'd been able to fall asleep following the episode—the *latest* episode in the Rook and Viva Show. Unfortunately, she'd awakened after way too few hours of total oblivion. Accepting that additional sleep would not be forthcoming, she performed the morning rituals of washing her face and brushing her teeth. Her plan was to settle back into bed and review the script she'd brought along until she was sure Rook had left the suite to begin his day.

She'd read through three scenes, when knocking sounded at the bedroom door. Rook opened it without waiting on her permission to enter. He stood leaning on the jamb with an amused, knowing smile softening the brutal handsomeness of his face.

"Do diva actresses have something against serving themselves breakfast?" he asked.

Viva continued studying her script, hoping he couldn't see how badly her hands shook. His voice practically reverberated in the room. The effect sent her heart thudding to her throat.

"No," she said with a coolness she didn't at all feel, "but they do find it difficult to stomach breakfast in the presence of cowards."

The word was as stinging as it was unexpected. Rook's reaction to it played all over his expression and he couldn't seem to suppress it.

"Coward?" He gave in to a few seconds of silence before reiterating the insult.

"Mmm..." Viva confirmed, continuing to idly flip through the script.

Rook's chest expanded as he took deep breaths to induce a calm he desperately wanted to feel. He'd expected to hear her call him almost anything but a coward.

"In what way?" He braced himself for her response. She didn't give him the benefit of eye contact.

"You're a smart man, Rook. I don't think an explanation is necessary."

"Maybe not, but why don't you give me one anyway?"

Viva at last put down the script and observed him with bold interest while he stood with his arms folded across his stunning chest.

"So let me get this straight," she began. "*I'm* required to provide explanations while you…get to duck and dodge them like…I don't know…a coward?"

Rook betrayed that the word stung him a second time by giving in to a reflexive jerk of his shoulders beneath the black fleece sweatshirt he wore over a denim shirt of the same color. "Does it matter that I plan to talk through this once we get back to Philly?"

"Ahh…so you're just *afraid* to talk to me *here*?"

"Don't push me, V."

"Rook," she said as she scooted to her knees in the bed, "what's going on with you?" Concern had overruled her anger or the need to pout. "What do all these little comments really mean?" She rolled her eyes and flopped back to the bed while waving off the sigh he uttered in response. "I know, I know…you can't talk about it *here*."

"This isn't easy for me, Viva."

"And you think it's easy for me?" she cried, inwardly cringing at the loss of composure. "There're things you need to know, Rook. Things I need— *want*—to tell you and I—I've waited too long to." She studied her palms as if they held answers to a puzzle she was desperate to solve. "It was easy to live with that when we were on opposite coasts. Just know, Rook, it's as hard for me to keep quiet as it is for you to talk."

She shook her head then, mutinous fire turning her gaze to molten chocolate. "At least *I'm* willing to get over myself and try to get through it."

Rook pushed off the doorjamb then. "This is about more than the two of us trying to get closure over some old drama. You'll have to excuse me if this isn't as *easy* for me as it is for you—"

Viva shoved off the bed and charged. "Damn you, Rook." She shoved at his chest once, then again. Her anger skyrocketed when the push didn't even cause him to stumble.

"Go to hell," she breathed and then gave a regal turn to settle back against the decadent king bed. "Take your cowardice issues with you." She prepared to delve back into her script.

Moments later, the item was yanked from her hands and Viva watched it sail across the room. Her eyes flew to Rook's and she was struck by the raw hunger she found there. She knew what came next—and she welcomed it. He'd be in for a different finale this time, she promised herself.

Rook made good on what his gaze promised. He made no attempt to mask his intentions from Viva. Frustration had all but consumed him. He was a man used to having his plans adhered to and going off without incident. It was what made him such a success in his business.

This wasn't business though. It was a matter all too personal. He'd wanted to hash out everything between them and then have them retreat to their opposing corners for reflection.

Circumstances hadn't allowed for that, however, and now they were in the midst of tension, with her believing him to be a coward of all things. Yes, frustration was tormenting him like a wound rubbed raw and refusing to heal.

Like some injured creature seeking solace from the pain, he was ready to pounce on anything that could prevent it. With the script hurled off to parts unknown, next was the scrap of cotton that had served as Viva's sleep attire the night before.

He had her naked within seconds. But for her heaving breasts and the malice spewing from her dark eyes, she made no other movements.

Rook appreciated the silence challenge.

Chapter 9

Aside from an almost inaudible grunt of surprise, Viva gave no other reaction to Rook's touch. Her nightgown was gone and he'd jerked her down toward the edge of the bed, his fingers curling into the side stitching of her panties. Determined, she refused to give him the satisfaction of letting him see her blink in response as he tugged her free of the delicate white lace. Her eyes remained fixed on his though. The look was challenging and yes, accusing even in their coolness.

Once he'd freed her of the undergarments, Rook tossed them aside as carelessly as he had the script and her sleepwear. Palming her bare hips, he then eased around to knead her lush bottom.

Viva couldn't resist blinking then as she swallowed noticeably. Her heart gave a reactionary lilt when he tugged her closer to the edge of the bed as he knelt there. For long moments, he studied her, his eyes slowly tracking her with desire continuously darkening his vivid stare.

"Coward," she breathed, though the insult had lost much of its kick.

"Right." His voice was a guttural slur as he dipped his head to pamper her inner thighs with firm strokes from the tip of his nose.

Viva bit her lip to resist flinching when his probing reached the folds of her center. There, he skimmed the velvety flesh and inhaled her arousing scent.

"Coward—" She verbalized the taunt again only to have it cut abruptly short when his tongue teased apart her intimate folds and lightly explored the treasure beyond. A shudder rippled through her and she fisted the tangled linens as she cursed her reaction to him. No longer could she deny her need to moan. She gave in to a long, quivering one when his tongue lengthened its exploration into her tight, hot, wet core.

Her hips began a slow writhe only to be stifled from movement when he held her fast and feasted. She melted into the covers, dragging her fingers through her hair and faintly rocking her hips in time to the rhythm he set with his skillful tongue.

Waves of orgasmic pressure turned her into a creature of need, one bent on achieving one goal—pleasure. Rook's head moved this way and that as he alternated speed and deepened penetration. Tentatively, she dropped her hand to trail over the sleek cap of his hair and was further stimulated by the feel of his head bumping her palms.

She tried to speak his name, but the attempt resulted in only a garble of sound. Rook was taking his task seriously, kneading her thighs and keeping them spread to accommodate the breadth of his frame.

Viva continued to melt into the bedding. Orgasm was a fervent pursuer and she was suspended between wanting to deny its effects and totally oblige them. Surrender, she feared, could result in having the man she desired withdraw far too soon. Satisfaction gripped her like a vise then, sending her breath shaking. Renewed spasms jolted, spewing fiery tingles along her nerve endings. She embraced them like the missed sensations they were.

Rook was in tune to her reactions as usual. Slowly he withdrew, but it was only to kiss his way up along her damp skin until he was outlining her breasts with his tongue. He abandoned them though, preferring the sweetness of her mouth. He kissed her, plundering her mouth as thoroughly as he had the rest of her.

Viva accepted the kiss enthusiastically as she attempted to draw every ounce of her taste from his tongue. Her efforts cooled as she achieved her goal. Then, it was on to her next feat.

She had to stifle a smile when she took advantage of Rook's loosened hold. Suddenly, she shoved him off her, and saw his eyes flare with disbelief and simmering temper.

"Thank you for this. It took the edge off." She scanned the bed and then pinned him with a coy look. "But we both know you aren't going to finish what you start and I'm in no mood to be…frustrated again."

Showing off her agility, Viva scooted from under him and rolled to the other side of the bed to lie on her stomach. "Shut the door on your way out, will you?"

Rook's surprise over her sudden turn of the tables had begun to wane. Even his temper—only a subtle flare—had eased back. Frustration, however, had continued to rage hot and heavily. He stood then, watching as Viva lay there, a curvy, caramel-doused picture. She lounged at length, as though she had no care for the state she was leaving him in. He couldn't blame her for torturing him as she was. With that thought in mind, he turned to the door.

Viva heard the slam behind her and fought the urge to curse and plant a fist to the bed. Before she could fully wallow in disappointment over calling his bluff, she felt his crushing weight at her back. Heat engulfed her at once. Rook's mouth was everywhere, skimming her nape, the tops of her shoulders, her spine, his tongue feverishly grazing its dip before he nibbled at the rise of her buttocks. All the while, he tugged the shirt from his back.

Viva arched in reflex, not expecting the path his wicked tongue took as he reacquainted itself with her derriere. Sheer delight had her smiling and softly moaning in high approval of him taking possession of her hips to hold her still for his exploration.

Maintaining that hold, Rook shifted Viva beneath the erotic pressure his mouth delivered. His fingers were just as busy, tormenting her sex with the gentlest caresses before lunging high and deep to become immersed in the moisture there.

Viva turned her face into the nearest pillow and moaned. Rook's beautiful mouth was then at work nibbling the spot where cheek merged with thigh. All the while, his persuasive fingers continued their lusty invasion of her femininity.

"Rook." His name was wrapped up in a shuddering moan.

"Save it." His voice was still little more than a guttural whisper.

Still, Viva pleaded as another climax loomed dangerously close. She didn't want that—not yet anyway. She wanted more of him and tried to relay that need through the insistent nudges she made against the erection straining the button fly of his denims.

She whimpered and he, at last, acquiesced. Viva sighed when his fingers withdrew. Disappointment surged as did delight when she felt his hand braced against the small of her back as he opened his jeans. Elation wrapped over that delight when she felt the proof of his need for her resting heavily at her spine.

Viva moaned, hungrily accepting the crushing kiss Rook subjected her to once he cupped her jaw and angled her to receive it. She had no issue with him taking such thorough command, especially when he traded his hold on her face for one at her breast. She smiled, content and in awe of the unmatched pleasure he could create with the simplest touch. She did squirm though, when he left her breast bereft of further exploration.

Mounting impatience gave way to extreme approval when Viva heard the distinct rip of condom packaging. Smiling, she snuggled her face into a pillow.

"You came prepared," she purred.

"It's why I came over here in the first place. Now shut up." His voice was gruff, yet playful.

Viva had only enough time for a single lilt of laughter before Rook's hands were once again smothering her hips and positioning her to take him from behind. Her gasp hinged on a shriek of welcome when he filled her. Instantly, he was stretching her, hastening the climax within a few potent strokes.

"V? Is it too much?"

The query was quiet and given in a manner so sweet, she could've sobbed from the pleasure it added to the moment.

"Yes," she admitted, arching back to take all he had to give. "And if you stop, I'll kill you."

Contentment was like warm syrup gliding through her veins when she felt his chuckles vibrate into her back. That feeling, combined with what he was doing to the rest of her body... Viva didn't think she could hold out against giving herself completely over to it.

"Not yet," he murmured into her hair where he'd buried his face to inhale the fragrance clinging to her coiled tresses.

"Not yet," he repeated, lightly gnawing her shoulder. His perfect teeth grazed the silken flesh he found there.

One big hand remained secure about her thigh, keeping her positioned to enjoy the full extent of his penetration. His other hand had expertly snaked beneath her to once again cradle a pouting breast.

Unashamed and overwhelmed, Viva whimpered as the barrage of sensation claimed her sex. She'd missed him so—his size, the mastery of his hard, big body...

"Not yet, V, please..." Rook could tell she was at her limit in the way her muscles clenched and held him. "Not yet," he chanted as he exquisitely, expertly, incomparably claimed her.

"Not yet," he directed even as he lost control over his restraint and spilled his seed into the condom's thin sheath. Around him, he could feel her sex squeezing his with an almost painful intensity.

The room filled with the sounds of mingled breathing then. Viva felt Rook shift behind her and withdraw once he was spent. Her contentment had no chance to wane, however, as he secured her in a spooning embrace. He kept her there as they drifted into a lengthy and restful doze.

Hours later, Viva woke to find herself tucked cozily beneath the covers. For an instant, she feared it had all been a dream. That was before she shifted on the bed and felt a wondrous discomfort lurking in her muscles and well-used sex. She wanted Rook back, but knew he'd gone to at last get started on his day. It was his real reason for being there, after all.

Yawning, she took a moment to get her bearings and did a bit of quick math in her head. Then, she was reaching for the phone to dial her sister. She estimated it was about 5:00 a.m. in Philadelphia and hoped to get Sophia's voice mail. She wasn't at all surprised when the driven detective answered after three rings.

Sophia laughed. "Lucky for me it's a busy week for both of us. We're trying to wrap up some stuff before the wedding."

"In that case you're forgiven."

"So…" It was Sophia's turn to tease. "Don't you have a soon-to-be-ex ex you need to be smoothing things over with?"

Viva laughed, enjoying the remark. "We're working on it."

"I see… So? Can you share or are the details too obscene?"

"Mmm…" Viva languished between the covers and smiled wickedly. "They may be a bit too…explicit to share over international airspace."

Sophia screamed and Viva basked in her sister's approval before reality set in. "We didn't get around to discussing anything we needed to, Soap."

"Aw, girl, don't be so hard on yourself. Maybe this way you guys can hear each other without all the other…tension getting in the way."

"Here's hoping," Viva sighed. "Sophia, he doesn't seem to want to discuss any part of what went wrong."

"Why do you think that is?"

"He says he *can't* talk about it."

"Can't?"

"Mmm…"

"Well, maybe—" Sophia piped up seconds before shutting herself down.

"Exactly." Viva wasn't surprised by her sister's inability to come up with something to explain Rook's outlook.

"Listen, V, just forget it for now and focus on the bright side. You've gotten closer physically at least. It shouldn't be…*too* hard to enjoy that part."

"Hmm…" Viva adopted some of her sister's light manner. "You could have a point. I guess I could *force* myself to enjoy it." She joined in when Sophia dissolved into a fit of giggling.

"So have you talked to Rook since we left?" Viva was asking a short while later.

"No, why?"

Bracing herself, Viva shared the news about her friend and cast mate Bevy Ward.

"Glad I used my head and insisted on Rook taking

you with him," Sophia quietly complimented herself once Viva had completed her recap.

"It could still be a coincidence, you know?"

"V, come on. You don't believe that any more than Rook does."

"Yeah, well…" Viva began to rub at the sudden pressure along the bridge of her nose. "He doesn't even want to hear me say that this doesn't sound like the kind of thing Murray would do."

"Maybe you're a little too close to Murray to see that it could be."

"I can accept that, Sophia. It's just…a larger part won't let me believe it."

"A person can be capable of all kinds of things if their back is pushed hard enough against a wall." Sophia expressed the observation quietly, as though she knew she was treading on delicate waters.

"I can accept that too, Sophia. Just please don't close yourself off to the possibility that there could be some other explanation for these strange coincidences." Viva pushed up in the bed, "Sophia, promise to keep an open mind on that. There're tons of crimes that go unsolved because the police close themselves off to considering any other explanations aside from the ones *they* want to patronize."

"I got it, I got it and I won't even give you a hard time about preaching since you're a taxpayer."

"Hmph, thanks." Viva realized how rattled she'd become and settled back to the bed. "I'm sorry, Soap. I know Murray's got no one to blame but himself for what's happening, but attacking people who make him money… Well, it just seems weird."

"Have more people than you seen him associating

with folks he shouldn't have been?" Sophia sighed when quiet greeted her question. "Look, *I'll* keep an open mind about Murray, so long as *you* keep an open mind that the possibility exists that he just might try to silence those who could help seal his fate in a not-so-good way."

"I will." Viva gave up trying to massage away the ache between her brows. It was there to stay. "Thanks, Soap. I love you."

"Love you too. Talk to you soon."

Once the connection ended, Viva took a moment to silently rehash the conversation. The endeavor was brief as she was soon shaking her head to ward off the jousting match between her opinion and her sister's.

Viva was inching out from beneath the covers, when she heard a door close near the front of the suite. "Rook?" she called, enjoying the shiver that streaked along her spine when he responded.

When he arrived in her doorway, it was to give her a playfully scrutinizing look. "Still in bed? You're taking this jet-lag thing a bit far."

Viva languished back once more. "I thought you'd be gone longer."

"Disappointed?"

"Mmm…no…" She let her lashes flutter as if she were in the midst of savoring a treat or a memory. "Nope…it's not disappointment I'm feeling. Can you come back to bed?"

His resulting smile expressed distinct regret. "We should get a move on if we plan to make it to Cortina by dark.

"I'm gonna get you settled out there and then come

back to get things started. I'll be back every night before dark though."

Viva didn't want to give in to the twinges of agitation his words stirred, but she couldn't help it. "You'll be back before dark every night, but you'll make sure I'm fast asleep before you head for bed, right?"

"Has anything I've said to you mattered, V?" He sighed. "This talk you want to have so bad? We'll have it when we're back and that's it."

"And does it matter to you that it's hard to be around you with this between us like some elephant in the room? What if it was just me talking?" Her gaze was as pleading as the hitch in her voice. "You could save your rebuttal for when we're back."

"Why's this so important to you after all this time?" He shoved off the door frame with noticeable force. "Yes, it's crazy with us all of a sudden being around each other like this, but—"

"You were right," she blurted with a defiant shake of her head that sent the light brown curls flying into her pretty face. "You were right about everything— just like my parents were right. Everything you tried to warn me I was letting myself in for with Murray and this life…" She lifted her hands, let them fall back to the covers in defeat.

Rook had gone rigid. His bright eyes were fixed and more riveting given the intensity of his stare.

Viva averted her gaze, deciding that *not* looking at Rook would keep her talking a lot longer. Judging from the look on his face, she thought he seemed quite interested in what she had to say. Finally.

"Everything you guys warned me would happen… it wasn't all bold and in my face, it—it was all very subtle and after a while I started to think that it really was just all of you trying to stifle me, not wanting me to go after my dreams, to stay where you wanted me, live the dreams *you* had for me." She rolled her eyes wearily and shrugged.

"I forgot all the warnings and let myself be wooed into the life. It wasn't hard. I'd have found a way in even if I hadn't been wooed. But I was and I accepted it all so greedily and then…it was time to prove how much I really wanted it."

Rook could feel the heat rising at his collar to begin a slow but steady streak across his nape. Not a good sign. "We can finish this later, V."

Her head snapped up, eyes flying to his face with pleading intensity. "Rook—"

"Later." He was backing out the door.

"Vossler." The name was soft on her lips, but she knew he heard her when he stopped moving toward the door. "I slept with him."

Rook hung his head, defeat claiming him then, as well. "I'm gonna take a wild stab and guess it wasn't hard for you to be wooed into that either?"

She bristled but accepted the blow and ached as though she'd expected it and needed it.

"Did it make you feel better to tell me that, V?" He moved back into the room. "Did you think it'd give me some kind of sick kick to hear I'd been right about that? About *that* of all things?"

She felt chilled then, not so much by the state of her undress as she was by the monotone of his voice. "I don't know why I told you…only that for so long I felt like I needed to."

"To ease your guilt."

"Maybe."

He was quiet for a long while, smoothing his thumb across the lines in his palm. "I can't speak to your family's motives for saying the things they did to keep you from leaving, V, but I can speak to my own." He waited for her eyes to meet his. "I was grabbing at anything to keep you where you were—that part's true. But it wasn't so you could live by my rules. It was because I knew that where you were going, there'd be no one to look out for you the way that I could."

Viva scooted to her knees and refreshed the pleading warmth of her gaze. "I know you have your problems with Murray, but I need you to know he did right by me. He looked out for me. None of what happened was his fault. I made my own decisions. They were horrible, but they were my own."

Rook grinned, but anger dwelled heavily in his eyes. "Murray Dean can do no wrong by you, can he?"

"Rook—"

"I already knew about Vossler. Maybe when you jump down off the Murray bandwagon you'll ask yourself how it is that I found out." He closed his hand over the doorknob. "Get dressed. We're out in an hour."

The chill attacking Viva's bare skin had her shivering blatantly before the door closed behind Rook.

Chapter 10

"It's furnished, but I'm not sure how much of a home it is."

Viva preceded Rook through a pair of double oak doors that pretty much dwarfed her. The remarks about his new acquisition had no effect on her.

In her opinion, the two-story chalet gave off an unarguably homey feel. Viva moved slowly through the lower level, her gloved hands reverently tracing the polished wood surfaces of the bookshelves, message and end tables as well as the rounded cushions of the sofas and armchairs furnishing the sitting room.

"It's beautiful," she said, her voice quiet, awed. "Looks like someone's already made a home of it."

Rook was preoccupied with bringing in the luggage from the stone entryway leading to a wide maple-paneled corridor. He seemed too involved in his task to take time to soak in the allure of his new digs.

"The previous owners threw in the furniture," he spared a moment to tell her. "The wife's uncle passed away and left her a fully furnished villa in Morocco or something."

"Nice." Viva's mouth turned down into an impressed smile as she resumed her inspection of the elegant surroundings.

To herself, she noted that the place really only needed a few personal touches to give it a bit of extra warmth. She turned to eye Rook when he entered the room and watched as he shook faint sprinkles of snowfall from the charcoal-brown bomber jacket he wore.

"You made a great choice." She complimented the house when he caught her staring.

Rook took a moment to look around the room as well. "We'll see." His grim tone matched the cool look he directed her way. He motioned toward the ceiling. "Go pick out your room—there're six of them. You're welcome to the master. The others can comfortably sleep up to three grown men."

Viva tried to appreciate his words with a smile, but the effort took its toll. The easily delivered instructions answered one question—they wouldn't be sharing a room. She decided not to waste time berating herself for insisting on sharing past information they both could've done without hearing—or hearing again. He already knew. He knew! Murray had told him…

She shook her head, hoping it hadn't become too

obvious that she'd gotten lost in her thoughts. "You should at least have the master," she urged in a breezy tone.

"I'll have my pick soon enough." Rook headed across the room to stoop before a massive hearth that was framed with hand-carved stone. There, he inspected the screen and wrought-iron fireplace tools set to one side of the long brick foundation.

Viva took pride in not bristling that time. She'd received the answer to yet another question. He was more than ready to be rid of her.

Rook must've sensed how hastily his words came across, for he bowed his head and stood as if the effort weighed heavily upon him. "Chances are I won't have much time to sleep between working and commuting between here and Belluno."

Viva went to the frost-crusted doors leading out to a wraparound balcony. "Why'd you pick this location? It's so remote..." As she studied the range of snowy mountains, her voice turned dreamy.

Rook's tone sounded much the same when he responded. "I think that's why. The agent just showed it to me on the fly." He moved to join Viva at the doors and savored the breathtaking view, as well.

"When I saw it, I thought I could actually *feel* the quiet." The idea had him grinning and he shrugged. "I was sold."

"I believe you." Her eyes were still fixed on the view.

Silence held between them for a time. It was a comfortable quiet in spite of all that had been said.

"Rook—"

He moved suddenly, the sound of her voice seeming to galvanize him into action. "Let me know when you've decided on that room," he said and quickly left her.

Viva soon learned that she was to be left to her own devices. Rook may not have spent much time soaking in all the comfort and solace his new home had to offer, but he had certainly devoted a great deal of time to outfitting its security measures.

Cameras were fixed to every entrance, from those nearest the house to the farthest reaches of the property. There were motion and even heat sensors. The local authorities were but a phone button's push away. They were in such close proximity that Rook didn't feel too agitated over the idea of leaving Viva while he tended to business outside of town.

When Viva teased him that morning about her surprise over him not having a stone fence erected around the property, he grimly confessed that he'd wanted to but was told such a thing would ruin the aesthetics of the landscape. They had shared a quick laugh over the remark, but nothing more. Rook made a hasty departure soon after.

She considered calling Sophia to vent, but decided the woman had far more important things to keep her mind occupied than helping her big sister unravel her affairs of the heart. Besides, it was a priority that whoever was responsible for Bevy's accident and, she suspected, Reynolds Henry's death be stopped.

In spite of everything, she just couldn't make herself believe that Murray was at the bottom of it all. She winced then at the echo of a quiet voice in the back of her mind. The voice was calling her a fool of the highest caliber.

Hadn't she been a witness to what Murray was becoming long before Sophia's investigation put a spotlight on him? Hadn't Rook just confirmed the lengths he'd gone to to ensure the final and immovable nail had been driven into the coffin of their relationship? All that and still she wouldn't believe that Murray Dean had crossed over the line from petty security specialist to something more…monstrous.

"Stop it, Viva. Focus, dammit." She felt a measure of accomplishment when the sound of her voice muffled the one in her head. There was more to occupy her time than thoughts of Murray. She had the script and intimidating six-inch stilts still demanding her mastery.

Those tasks however, weren't nearly as appealing to her as exploring and possibly enhancing her new surroundings. If she was lucky, she mused, she might "enhance" well enough to bring a smile of approval to her host's handsome face. She wouldn't hold out much hope for that though. At the very least, devoting her time to taking on the role of homemaker would perhaps take her mind off what was or *wasn't* happening with her and Rook.

She'd found the chalet to be quite inviting upon first glance. It needed only a few creative accents to add the warmth that shrieked welcome. Viva spent much of the morning roaming the rustic oasis of stone, marble and wood. Windows were in high supply with flower boxes enhancing each of the rectangular holders along the sills. She could almost envision the colorful flora indigenous to the area filling each of the maple boxes with splashes of vibrant color once spring began to grace the environment with new signs of life.

For now, no such enhancements were possible save those of a more man-made variety. Viva went to work on the lamps. Already, she imagined their golden glow filtering out of the numerous windows to give the place the look of a gleaming destination in the midst of a quiet wonderland. The chandeliers were both elegant and unique as they hung from the wood-beamed ceilings of most every room. Still, Viva preferred the cozy invitation only a lamp could offer.

She took advantage of a surprisingly dependable Wi-Fi connection and checked the sites of several local shops. By day's end, she'd put in orders for window treatments and various bathroom accents. One of the shops delivered the first shipment of lamps. The vans were thoroughly checked by the two-man/two-woman security team at the main road. Viva had ordered for the downstairs rooms as well as the two bedrooms she and Rook had claimed. Additional items would arrive over the course of the week and she was certain that her brooding host would notice the minor transformation when he returned.

The hour-and-fifteen-minute commute between Cortina and Belluno gave Rook the time to both clear his mind and return it to its state of cluttered chaos. Luckily, the clearing had taken place as he'd made his way in to meet with the personnel of his European offices and the exclusive clientele he'd be serving there once the deal was closed. The day had been a fast-paced and productive one. So much so, Rook found himself taking the access road to the chalet before the full black of night had descended.

Rook had made small talk with the second shift guard detail and had been surprised, yet pleased to hear about all the activity that had taken place. With any luck, the fact that Viva was making herself at home was a hopeful sign that they could spend more time enjoying the tranquility of his newfound digs instead of the consistent argument about issues long past.

He pulled the Range Rover to a stop several feet from the chalet's main entrance and simply stared. Every window glowed golden bright, a radiant sight against the early evening skies of blues, purples and pinks tinting the horizon to usher in dusk. Easing up on the brakes, he advanced slowly, still in awe of the transformation.

Until that evening, he'd only seen the place lit by the motion and porch lighting, with scant illumination from the indoors. It was a stunning sight. It was the sight of home.

"Guess it's real now," he said to the empty car interior and thought of what that meant.

He wasn't afraid that he wouldn't see his family and friends on a regular basis. He thought of what a kick his mother would get out of telling her friends that she and his dad would be vacationing in Northern Italy. As for Elias and the guys—they were like his brothers. It'd take a lot more than a move halfway around the world to change that.

No, his concern was for Viva. True, things had long since ended between them… He shook his head free of the vivid imagery of them making love less than twenty-four hours ago. Despite that, things between them had ended long ago, but he'd never sensed the finality of it until that moment.

This move to Italy put a new turn on things entirely. After all, there wouldn't be much of a possibility for him to run into her while she was back visiting her parents, would there? Forget living on different coasts, they'd be living in different countries.

"What a mess." He smoothed a hand over his hair and grimaced. He'd finally gotten the courage to begin cutting emotional ties and they instantly engaged to snare him like vises.

Rook shut down the SUV and covered the rest of the gravel drive on foot. Upon entering the house, he reset the security code and was about to call out to Viva when he heard her outburst.

"If you want to fix things between us, this isn't the way!… I don't give a damn if you don't approve. This is my job… Please don't be that way… I didn't ask you here to fight…"

"V?" Frowning, Rook took steady yet cautious steps down the gleaming cobblestone floors of the main corridor. He peeked into the sitting room and the living room, before he found Viva in the den at the rear of the lower level. Discovery dawned and with it came the complete removal of the darkness that had dominated his expression for the better part of the day.

Viva stood in the middle of the den. The room gleamed golden thanks to the newly placed lamps dotting the stout oak end tables flanking thickly cushioned armchairs with their carefully crafted plum upholstery. She held on to a sheaf of papers that Rook immediately identified as her new script and the reason for her intermittent outburst fell into place.

Bracing a shoulder to the den's open doorway, Rook settled in for the show. It was a treat for sure and in more ways than one. The performance was one-sided, but Viva threw a vibrancy into every passage she uttered. It was a chore to look away from her on-screen, he thought. In person, looking away was a futile endeavor for a mere man. It wasn't only a futile endeavor, it was an insane one.

The caramel-toned beauty strutted around in a T-shirt, skintight capri yoga pants and what had to be eight-inch heels like she'd been born in them. Rook inhaled deeply, but kept the intake as soft as he did the exhale while he watched her saunter toward one of the coffee-brown sofas. Somehow, he managed to keep his mouth from dropping open when she plopped down on the sofa in a straddling position and faced the back of the chair.

She kept her eyes on the script and had yet to notice him there using the door frame to support his weight as his legs had become unable to. Viva put her free hand to the sofa, smoothing at the suede with the back of her hand as she might smooth the skin of her lover. Vivid imagery slashed through his mind again and it was he who benefited from the touch he watched her give the sofa with mutinous envy.

The sound of an unintended groan filling the air gave Viva a start and she scooted round on the sofa to find Rook there. Though she was flustered, a slight trace of the practiced naughtiness she'd conjured for the scene still shone through.

"Looks like you've mastered the shoes," Rook said.

Swallowing noticeably, Viva cast a withering look toward the spike-heeled violet satin pumps. The shoes hugged her instep as adoringly as the black and violet ties did her shapely calves.

"It's all about the attitude." The shrug she gave harbored the same withering manner. "Once you master that, the rest is easy."

"If you say so." His stirring eyes traversed the pumps with lingering approval.

"Sorry, I must've lost track of time," she said before their silence grew strained. "I could've done this in my room." She waved the script.

Rook moved from the doorway. "I'd be a fool if I said this wasn't a nice sight to come home to." *Nice.* He silently turned the word over in his head. It was erotic at its finest.

Viva gave a wistful smile then as she scanned the golden-lit room. "I could've saved myself the trouble of all the lamps."

"Glad you didn't." He took the time to observe his den as he moved deeper into the room. "It all hit me as soon as I took the road in. Felt like home."

"Well, then." Viva spread her arms and let her hands fall back to her sides. Her expressive stare pooled with pride and delight. "Guess I accomplished my mission to do at least *that* much." Another goal of that mission had been to improve his mood. As yet, she'd been unable to get a better bead on whether she'd managed that.

Rook moved to join her on the sofa and she scooted to make room.

"That looked like some scene," he said as he nodded toward the script.

"Uh, yeah." Viva ignored the burn in her cheeks. "It's harder when you have to play it alone."

"Trouble in paradise?"

She knew what he meant, and smiled. "Not yet, but the writers are pushing for it so…it's coming."

"So what's up?" He tugged the edge of the script she'd set on the cushion between them. He regarded her slyly. "Or is it a secret?"

She gave in to a more pronounced smile. "I guess I can dish a little." Her expression sobered when she looked to the script. "Leesi's trying to convince Cabot to do something he doesn't want to do," she shared, referring to her on-screen love Cabot Ryan, who was played by Bryce Danzig.

"And what is it that he doesn't want to do?"

"Let her go." Viva watched the muscle flex along his jaw, a reaction she'd anticipated.

"Why would she want him to do that?" Rook's gaze fixed upon the script. His voice had gone softer.

Viva chose to keep her eyes on his killer face instead. "She's got a job to do and she knows he won't be able to handle what she'll have to do to get it done."

Rook responded with a solemn nod. "Maybe he could."

"He'll believe that—for a while."

"So that's it? She'll just assume—"

"She's not assuming. She's got years of their relationship giving her all the material she needs to come to a very informed conclusion."

"So much material that she won't even give him a chance to fix it?"

"She *is* giving him a chance."

"How?" He gave her the benefit of eye contact then. "By asking him to let her go?"

Viva looked to the script then. "I think she hopes he'll follow her. I don't think she even knows that's what she wants, but it is."

"That's a risky game she's playing. They could lose each other for years. Anything could hap—" Rook cut his words short, just as Viva's sharp intake of breath filled the room.

With another shaky breath, she started to shove off the sofa. Rook caught her wrist before she'd done little more than press her hand into the cushions. An instant later, she found herself positioned as she had been while running lines with her imaginary co-star. But this time her knees were planted on either side of Rook's hips, and she knew she had no other choice but to look directly into his exceptional face.

Helplessly, her eyes lowered to his mouth, and memories of its talents shot a blunt throb of need through her core. Reflexively, she moistened her bottom lip and saw the move draw his bright stare to the location.

He stared for a time as though transfixed by the way the pink tip of her tongue darted out to travel across the lush lips accentuated by a light bronze glosser. The sound of his name whispering past them was his undoing.

The hand cupping her hip made a quick ascent until it rested between Viva's shoulder blades. He brought her in closer until he was crushing her velvety mouth against his hard one. Her gasp granted greater depth for his tongue to explore and he did so with sheer relish fueling his moves.

Her hands were weak, yet she just managed to curl them around the lapels of the quarter-length wool jacket he'd yet to remove. Strength may have left her hands but the same couldn't be said of her kiss. Eagerness flooded the gesture to rule choice parts of her anatomy. Gently, she rocked her hips, performing a subtle grind against the ridge of his sex beneath a straining zipper. She moaned while she snuggled deeper into what she craved.

She was on the cusp of begging him to give her more, but her mouth was totally occupied with kissing and not talking. Blindly, her fingers glided from their grip around Rook's jacket lapels to unhook the top fastening of the slate-gray trousers he wore. She had nearly undone the fastening when he smothered her busy fingers beneath a big hand.

"Rook—" She got out just that much before he put her on her back in one seamless, rapid move.

Mouth freed, she begged in earnest then. He was plying the soft, fragrant column of her throat with gentle, wet kisses. Her breasts heaved with mounting vitality the nearer his talented and lovely mouth drew to them. When his lips merely skirted the tops, without so much as an outline around the nipples desperately straining against lacy bra cups, impatience had her cupping the back of his head to snare his sleek curls and offer encouragement.

She sobbed when he covered her free hand and squeezed in his own form of encouragement. Tears stung her eyes and she would've wrenched away, but he held her fast.

"I would've followed if you'd really wanted me to." He inched back when she ceased her struggling.

A mix of longing and regret rippled in his gaze before he squeezed her chin and smiled apologetically. "I would've followed, but you didn't want me to, V. Not then."

With that, he moved to leave her reeling in need and defeat.

Chapter 11

Over the two weeks that followed, Viva threw herself into every task and chore she could devise. Making Rook's house into a home had become less about fixing his mood, which she'd at last deemed a hopeless pursuit, and more about satisfying another personal longing.

The rustic, old-world dwelling underwent a gradual transformation that showcased Viva's flair for interior decorating as well as her love for cozy spaces that epitomized warmth and invitation.

Amid her decorating efforts, she mastered the script. She'd taken to practicing outside her room when Rook was gone, which was quite often. She told herself he had lots to do to get the new leg of his business up and running. That mind-set had sustained her for the first week but not so much going into the second.

She'd accepted that there was nothing she could do

to fix the new layer of trouble laid over their doomed relationship. Her dogged redecorating had been about living a fantasy—one that had not even a snowball's chance of becoming reality.

This was the life she wanted. She knew that. She had known that since long before circumstances had brought them back into one another's lives. He was right. She wouldn't have wanted him to come with her. Not then. Her career and the years she'd spent honing it were not things she resented.

Losing Rook in pursuit of it all, however… Yes, she greatly resented that. Now.

Viva tucked the black quilt beneath her neck and snuggled deeper into the den sofa where she'd lounged for much of the latter part of the afternoon. The snowfall had been a light, but steady drift that was hypnotic and a fabulous soother to her riotous thoughts.

She kept her mobile handy, dreading the call she had to make, but knowing it *had* to be made just the same. With any luck, her sister would be busy and she would get to leave the message she had rehearsed. As she reached for it in her back pocket, the phone jiggled, giving Viva a start. The name on the screen surprised her even as a welcoming grin spread across her face.

"Don't you have a broken leg and fractured collar bone to be mending? Or isn't there someone you should be ordering around? Maybe you're just trying to milk this bed-rest thing for as long as you can." Viva grinned while delivering the playful jibe.

Throaty laughter traveled through the line before an equally rich voice followed. "You know me so well.

I just sent Winnie to bring me a box of those cheese Danish from Reardon's."

"You should be ashamed." Viva shook her head while laughter tickled her throat. "Reardon's is on the other side of town from the hospital. What the hell time is it there anyway?"

"Hey! *She* wanted to!" Bevy Ward's attempt at whining came across instead as a wicked laugh. "Besides…" Her tone mellowed as she seemed to sober. "I needed some alone time to talk to you. Winnie was the only one still hovering and I needed her out."

"How are you, Bev? I know about the injuries."

"Yeah… I'm gonna be out of commission for a while." Hints of stress seeped into Bev's strong voice then. "Anyway… I guess there's a lot to be said for being in fair shape. Doctors are hopeful that the recovery won't be too agonizing. I'm fine though, trying to figure out who I've got to sleep with to keep a steady supply of these painkillers they're giving me. Those things are the ultimate."

Viva had to laugh over her friend's ability to apply comic relief in the direst of situations. "Good to know you've got goals."

"Exactly." Bevy grunted a laugh.

"So what's up?" Viva pushed up on the sofa and switched the phone to her other ear.

"Is it true, V?" Bevy wasted no more time getting to the point of her call. "What they're saying about Murray? Not that the cops are telling us anything," she continued, not noticing that Viva had yet to answer her questions.

"Arty told me they came to Murray's office," Bevy

went on. "She said they came with a warrant after what happened to Fee."

"Fee?" Viva sat all the way up on the sofa then as the image of Fee Fee Spikes began to form inside her head.

"You didn't hear about it yet?" The Southern accent Bevy worked doggedly to mask grew a little more noticeable as concern mounted. "Looks like Fee surprised a burglar and got a broken nose and a few cracked ribs out of the ordeal," she explained.

Viva muttered an oath. The bubbly redhead was a client of Murray Dean's.

"Anyway…" Bev grunted, as though she were moving to a more comfortable spot in her hospital bed. "They say she'll recover. Her manager and agent are screaming bloody murder though after what happened to Reynolds Henry and then me. They—they think someone could be targeting Murray's clients and the cops are hoping someone got a good look at the guy. We won't know till Fee wakes."

"The guy?" Viva gripped the slender mobile in a vise hold. "Not Murray?"

"Well…" Uncertainty filtered Bevy's reply. "I mean… I don't know what *they* think but—well… hell, V, it's *Murray*."

"Yeah…" Viva left the sofa, tugging at the hem of the T-shirt she'd sported with the hot-pink yoga shorts she'd worn that day. The apparel had pretty much become her primary wardrobe during her unexpected vacation abroad. "Yeah, it's Murray," she sighed.

"V? You don't think Murray—"

"No. No… *I* don't." Viva pushed back a few locks

of her hair and then pressed a finger to the corner of her eye to relieve the pressure building there. "My sister and Rook, on the other hand—"

"Rook?" The weary uncertainty that had gripped Bevy's voice made way for happy curiosity. "Well, well. So for once the gossip rags have it right? Talk about running off with an old flame... Is he as amazing looking as I've heard?"

The turn of conversation had heightened the pressure behind Viva's eyes and she was then massaging a sudden throb at the bridge of her nose. "Yes, he is."

"Weird." Bevy sighed. "Nothing popped off between you guys before as much as I've heard he works with folks in the business."

"Yeah." Viva gave up with the massage, realizing that it was useless. "Weird."

"So? What's it like? Talk to me."

Viva opened her mouth, then closed it. She could honestly offer nothing more to the conversation at that point.

"Ugghh..." Bevy noted from her end of the line. "That bad, huh? Or maybe that good?"

"Too much has happened, Bev. We can't go back to what we were."

"But you want to."

"It's too late."

"And is that what *he* thinks?"

"Our lives are crazy, Bev."

"Lives are always crazy, girl. Love though, *real* love? That shit only comes by once—or maybe twice—if you're lucky."

Viva had to smile then. "Are you biting off Pam's advice?"

Bevy sounded as though she were chuckling over the mention of her on-screen character. Apparently, she'd taken no offense to the accusation. "Hell, I don't see why not," she admitted. "It's damn good advice. Wouldn't hurt you to take it, you know."

"It's more than just a leap of faith here, Bev. He knows things that…they could change things…"

"Things that happened once you split, right?"

"He told me I'd get in over my head back then, Bev. I did."

"And you'll let that stop you from digging your way out?"

"He's made a life, Bev. A good one that's on its way to being a great one." Viva eyed the cozy room with a mix of envy and sadness. "I just had to go and open up all this old drama. It wasn't a good idea and it'll only distract him from what he has to do." She closed her eyes to the distant, snowy mountain view. "When all is said and done, he'll regret all the time he wasted and I'll still be who I am. Nothing there will have changed."

"Boy, you've really thought this through, huh?" Bev's voice held a hint of the playful. "You sound really sure of yourself."

Viva took a refreshing breath and managed a smile. "Nothing here to do but think."

"Well, Winnie should be back with those Danish soon and I think… I think your opinion is bullshit, V."

"Bev—"

"I'm gonna leave you to your thoughts. I think you

should take more time with them. Just call me if you have any more news from your end, okay?"

"All right and you do the same. And, Bev? Thanks."

"Love you, sweets."

"Love you too."

Viva didn't set aside the phone once the connection ended. Instead, she studied it, debating before she dialed out. Her lips thinned with resolve when she heard the voice mail chime through. "Soap? It's me. I need you to call me back when you get this."

"Catch you at a bad time?"

Rook barked a laugh when he heard Linus's query through the phone line. "That's one of those trick questions, right?"

"Ah, no…" Linus groaned, "please don't ruin my fantasies of what it must be like to have a Hollywood starlet all to yourself."

"All right, then." Rook let his silence do the talking.

Again, Linus groaned. "Are you serious here? You guys are a million miles away from everything."

Rook forced a smile, albeit a grim one. "I guess you can never outrun the past."

"Can't you at least set it aside to make room for better stuff?"

"Hell, man, do you think I don't want to? It's *all* I want. *She's* all I want." Tired of pretending his mind was on work, Rook hurled a pen across the desk. "Hollywood starlet or not, she's all I've *ever* wanted."

"So?" Linus let the challenge hold for a moment. "She's there, isn't she? My guess is she wouldn't have gone so quietly, or as quietly as she did, if part of her didn't want to. To hell with what Sophia dictated. Viva's got the means to disappear like that."

Rook heard the man's fingers snapping on the other end of the line.

"She came back for you, kid." Linus's voice was almost a whisper. "You should make use of that. You may not get another chance."

Rook left his desk to stare unseeingly beyond the office picture window that opened to a sea of white. "Maybe I don't think I deserve another chance."

"Bullshit."

"Oh, I get it." Rook turned his back on the snowy scene of the Belluno business park and evaluated his friend's assumption. "Is that what you tell yourself, Line? That all the crap you pulled in the name of having a reaction still means you get another chance? Is it so easy for you to forget that part of the past?" He pushed hard against the back of his desk chair when he passed and sent the furnishing spinning.

"You're right, it's all crap, but I'd take another chance again without hesitation if I had the opportunity to make it right. There's only one thing I regret enough to make the effort, you know? I believe Viva's that one thing for you and I believe you know that." When he only received silence as a response, Linus asked, "You should be getting home now, shouldn't you?"

Home. Rook turned the word over in his head. "Yeah, Line, home sound good."

Rook had been on his way out the door, with intentions to head home, when Linus's call had come through. The call had done a lot of good, despite his reluctance to hear much of his friend's insights. All he'd wanted was to forget; he didn't want to remember the man he'd been back then. The animal he'd been.

His fingers flexed over the steering wheel and he tried to give rising, unsettling memories a mental shove. Useless. There was no real forgetting them. Maybe the trick was to own the past. Viva had owned hers, hadn't she?

What mistakes had she really made though? He wondered. She'd gone after a dream and met up with some nightmares along the way. It wasn't an impossible occurrence. Such was often the case when one chased after the future.

The true mistakes had come in his reaction to what he'd learned. Now, the question was whether telling her about them was really necessary. He'd figured that was a yes, considering how poorly he'd dealt with it all since she'd come back into his life. *That* had roused her questions and she deserved answers—she deserved the truth.

Home appeared around the road's bend in all its welcoming splendor. As per usual when he got there, Rook took the time to just enjoy the view and gather the courage to face his demons. He parked, headed inside and was closing the door seconds before the sense of déjà vu washed over him.

"It's too much…I understand why you suggested it, but we need to find another way…No…No, it only went back to more drama…Don't worry about it, I'll figure something. I've got a costar in the hospital. Remember we told you about Bevy? I should spend time with her anyway. I need you with me on this, Soap. Being here with him is killing me…"

Rook eased the door locks quietly into place and then rested back against the wall as reality hit that this was no instance of déjà vu. He hadn't walked in on Viva rehearsing her script, but into the midst of a scene that was all too true to life. He waited just outside the den until Viva finished the call to her sister.

"Has my hospitality worn thin?"

She turned at the sound of Rook's voice when he entered the room.

"Don't bother using the injured costar excuse," he advised before she could answer. "I'd love to hear the reason you gave to Sophia."

Bowing her head, Viva pressed the tips of her fingers against eyes closed wearily in defeat. "I just don't know what we're doing here."

"I thought it was to save your life."

Her brows lifted as she smiled wistfully. "And does the 'save your life' rate include dynamic sex?"

He was, for a moment, silenced by the unexpected approval that surged in response to her backhanded compliment. He recovered soon enough. "You didn't seem to have a problem accepting the service."

The soft reminder prompted more than the nod she gave. "I hoped we were on our way back to each other."

The admission stopped him again. "You want that?"

She fixed him with a look that was as exasperated as it was accusing. "Of course I want that, you idiot.

I—" She squeezed her eyes shut once more, her cheeks burning over the unintended confession.

"Fortunately, dynamic sex isn't our problem," she professed once a sliver of cool had reasserted itself. "*Unfortunately*, we can't spend all our time in bed, which means at some point, we'll have to talk to each other." She extended her arms, let her hands fall to thighs bared by her shorts. "I don't think there's an argument on how bad we've been doing on that end."

"What does 'on our way back to each other' mean?" Rook was clearly still somewhat dazed by Viva's earlier admission. His rich voice sounded deeper given the soft-spoken manner it had adopted. His striking features were still sharp as he fixated upon her.

"Rook, you—you know what I meant—"

"I want to hear you say it." He closed what distance remained between them.

"Rook, I—I love you," she said quietly, helplessly, as though that single confession was all she was capable of. "I never stopped." She shook her head to put emphasis on the claim. "I want back what we had— what we could've had. I'm sorry I—" She blinked suddenly as though some part of her psyche were reconnecting to reality. "I didn't mean to put all that on you. I know things have changed and you—you can't…want me after I slept with—"

He'd gripped her so suddenly, she gave a tiny shriek before panting out a breath.

"Look at me, V."

For her, the effort was massive. She was close to paralyzed by uncertainty and…fear. Not fear of him, but fear of what she'd see in his eyes.

"Viva? Look at me." He squeezed the bend of her elbow and waited.

Drawing on practiced courage, she met his stunning eyes and gasped over what she saw there. There was no anger—not even a hint of frustration. What she saw instead was awe mingling with the brilliance of hope.

"Not wanting you isn't possible for me Viva. I don't know if it ever will be and I don't much care to find out."

Her lips parted, but Viva had no notion of what she was about to say. That wasn't a problem for Rook as he'd already found a task to occupy her mouth quite thoroughly.

The kiss was as needed as it was seeking. Rook's delivery was a hungry, possessive assault that had Viva instantly moaning and sobbing for more. She could scarcely curve her fingers into the lapels of the leather jacket he wore. No matter, for he kept her high against his chest in the most secure hold.

Needing to feel more of him, Viva wrapped her legs around his waist. Eagerly, she presented her mouth to be explored.

Rook felt as if he were roasting inside the wool lining of his jacket but he refused to relinquish his hold on Viva's bottom to get out of it. He had her flush between himself and the closest wall, in the span of two long strides.

"I'm sorry, sorry…" he groaned, while driving his tongue deep to savor the honeysuckle flavor of her mouth. His kiss drove her head back into the wall.

Viva didn't require apologies. She answered the rough treatment by stripping Rook, none too gently, of his brown jacket before she went to work on the dark shirt he wore beneath it. Silently, she warned herself not to rip the buttons free. Her fingers tingled with the need to stroke his bare flesh.

Those intentions took a backseat when his fingers slipped inside the snug crotch of her shorts. Simultaneous moans echoed in the room. Hers stimulated by his fingers inside her shorts. His by the fact that she wore nothing beneath them.

Rook let his forehead rest on her shoulder. He absorbed the shudders rippling through her curvy frame—a response to the erotic torment that stimulated moisture and held his fingers in the tight clench of her intimate muscles.

Viva found no need to hold on to his breathtaking shoulders. This, despite the fact that he only supported her with the forearm that cradled her bottom. She felt completely secure and she took advantage of that fact by focusing her efforts on the buttons yet to be undone. Once she had his shirt open, she splayed her hands upon the thick slabs of his muscular chest. Her lips were gliding down the chiseled length of his neck, across collarbone and sternum, until she was taking a pebbled male nipple into her mouth.

Rook grunted as sensation slammed into him. For several seconds he endured the pleasurable assault, then he was cursing viciously and bringing an end to the spectacular attention she was giving his chest.

"What?"

Her hushed query stirred his laughter and then he was kissing the corner of her mouth. "Come with me," he said.

* * *

Protection hadn't occurred to her. Viva wondered whether she'd have called attention to its absence if it had. Sure, there was lots more she wanted to do before she said goodbye to her career. Having Rook Lourdess's child was a choice she would have made her career work around.

"We could've stayed downstairs, you know?" She purred the words while tracking the end of her nose along his collarbone.

"We were missing some things," he said as he sheathed himself. Then he took her in his arms. A low sound of animalistic male pleasure thrummed from his throat as he took her with deliberate purpose.

Viva knew there was no need to muffle the sounds of her delight, yet she turned her face into a pillow anyway. She eased her hands beneath its cool cotton texture as her hips dipped and rolled to a rhythm honed by instinct, by want.

Another of Rook's quiet, satisfied rumbles emerged and his slow strokes were moments of pure bliss for Viva. She let out a choked sob when his beautifully shaped mouth took one nipple hostage in an achingly sweet suckle that sent need pooling between her thighs. Somehow, she held back the final barrier on her release.

She wanted more and wouldn't take for granted that what they shared in that moment would soon be repeated. Working then to, in some way, reciprocate his attention to her chest, she dragged a shaky hand up his sweat-slicked abs and rib cage until she was cupping a bulging pec. She caressed his nipple beneath her thumb.

Rook shuddered, his divine mouth still full of her breast. Viva seized the opportunity to turn the tables then and she had him on his back moments later. Their connection never broke; it had no chance to. Viva's hips were smothered in his hands, his hold so secure, it almost allowed for no movement.

Sensually slow, her body rocked in a fashion that sent orgasmic shudders ricocheting through her in thick, unapologetic waves. Her hands glided, coasting up her taut, trim torso. She made a brief stop to cup her breasts before moving on to drag her fingers through her hair and let the mass tumble around her enchanting face.

Rook received almost as much pleasure from the sight of her as he did from the feel of her squeezing the erection that showed no signs of losing its intensity anytime soon. When he sensed her needs were getting the better of her, he added more pressure to his hold at her hips in hopes of preventing her from taking him over the edge with her. Not yet, he told himself. Not yet.

Viva's shudders grew fiercer and Rook knew she was indeed at the limit of her resistance. He wanted more though and he meant to have it. Viva collapsed atop him, yet she still moved with an overt eroticism that would've made him come were it not for how greedy he still was for her.

Viva's smile reflected complete contentment. She felt oh so pampered when his lips brushed her brow for a tender kiss. Yes, she felt wholly content, or at least she *thought* she was, until he put her beneath him again.

This time, she was on her stomach with Rook's considerable weight more stimulating than it was crushing as he took her from behind. Spent as she was, Viva still latched onto a new wave of arousal. She arched up to receive him, gasping eagerly and panting while her intimate folds contracted in a desperate attempt to keep him still to savor.

Rook calmed his enthusiastic captive with quick, soft kisses to her ear and whispered, "Easy…it's my turn now…"

Chapter 12

"I was watching the show one night. You and what's his face were having…a moment."

Viva giggled. "Wholly content" seemed a poor way to describe the way she felt. While the sex had been supreme, the aftermath was hot on its heels. Snuggling into the perfection that was Rook's chest, she sent up a quick prayer for this time to be among the first of many.

"Bryce Danzig." She gave him the name of her leading man. "He's gay, you know?"

Rook snorted. "Hard to tell judging from his scenes with you."

Viva felt the urge to laugh again, knowing the emotion was brought on by more than Rook's teasing. It was from the true happiness coursing through her veins.

The only light glowed from the fireplace. The master suite was dark, even with the moon's illumination. It shone faint that night as it streamed in through windows yet to be covered by drawn drapes.

"Anyway…" Rook continued, snuggling his head deeper into the cradle provided by his arm tucked beneath it. "You were very into what he was doing and I…"

Viva pushed up on her elbow then to look down at him. "The show's director, Jake Hough, had to work a lot with us—me and Bryce—in the beginning. My acting experience was still very limited and Bryce's… sexual preference was a challenge. He'd never acted opposite a woman as a romantic lead before."

Viva rested back into the sheets when she saw she had Rook's attention. "Jake's advice to us was to see the person we most wanted to be with in the world. 'Every move you make, every sound you utter is for them,' he said." She grazed her knuckles against his jaw when he raised up over her.

"Every love scene I've ever done has been with you in my head," she said.

Rook's sly smile defined his features into a more devastating picture. "That was some pretty handy advice."

"Yes, yes, it was." Viva chuckled the words. "Hard to believe the man is four times divorced."

Laughter mingled with the pop and snap of the fire-engulfed logs in the hearth.

"That night I watched you with him," Rook continued, "and I heard you, um…responding to him. I thought about us, thought about you sounding that way for Vossler…and I lost it."

"Rook—" Viva didn't realize she was holding her

breath until he eased his staggering gaze her way. She didn't know what to say. There was no need for more.

"Let me finish," he soothed.

Viva allowed the breath she'd been holding to expel in a slow flow and somehow she managed to keep her gaze from faltering.

Rook sat up then, one arm hanging over a raised knee as he looked toward the fire. "My crew had been on a pretty rough case—it was a domestic thing. The client's daughter was trying to get out of a bad marriage. The ex rubbed the whole team the wrong way. The client hired us to watch her and make sure the fool didn't come around." He brought a hand to his jaw, massaged there for a moment as the buried memories began to surface.

"She'd served the jerk with papers the week before and her father—my client—wanted us to keep an eye out."

Viva decided to sit up then as well, but felt it best not to initiate contact. She could see the muscles in his wide back were rigid with tension.

"That night I saw you on TV...being there in the apartment, *our* apartment...it was too much." He squeezed his eyes shut, gave a quick shake of his head. "I went to relieve whomever was on shift. I just needed to get out of the house and take my mind off stuff—off you..." He passed Viva a sidelong smile, but didn't look her way.

"I went to the daughter's house, talked a little bit with my guys. I was going to take a walk around the grounds. My team was about to pull off when I heard her scream. It was a big place, so we didn't know how long he'd been in there with her before we heard her.

My people are obsessive about their jobs…" He shook his head again. "No way the bastard got past them, but there he was inside. Turned out, he talked his way in. Lied to her about wanting to put the past to rest— that's what she was able to tell me…later. Hmph…put *her* to rest was more like it. She was hurt pretty bad by the time we got him off her. My guys were calling the cops, so all I had to do was restrain him and let him cool his heels until they got there. I didn't."

Viva watched Rook's fists clench. She resisted drawing the sheets over her suddenly chilled skin.

"It just came over me," he said, and then studied his fists, as well. "Like a fever and I… I couldn't—" His sigh was loud over the wood crackling amid the fire.

"It's ironic." He laughed shortly, quietly then. "I beat the guy almost half to death—a guy who lost it when his ex just shook hands with another man and there *I* was on the verge of killing him because I couldn't handle seeing my—my ex…acting out a love scene."

"You know you were dealing with more than that." Viva tentatively voiced the reminder.

Rook angled his head, but still didn't give her the full benefit of his gaze. "It wasn't enough to justify what I did to that guy. No one blamed me for it, but they were plenty ready to lay blame by the end of a few more weeks. Thank God for Linus," he groaned, burying his face in his hands.

"Linus Brooks?" Viva frowned.

"He was the one who got me to include the fight-training service end to my business." He smirked. "Once I dealt with the crap load of anger that had me in danger of losing every friend I had in the world. I, um… I've come a long way on that end, but I've still got a long way to go. Which is why—"

"You kept giving me the brush-off on talking about it," she finished.

He smoothed both hands over his nape. "Right." He then worked the heels of his hands into his eyes while resting back onto the bed.

"So? What now?" Still sitting, Viva turned to study him where he lay.

Rook was quiet for a long time. "You have to know I tried everything to stay away from you. Over the years…there were a lot of times I could've changed that. I didn't and I'm sorry."

Viva returned the lopsided grin he sent her. "I could say the same, you know? What's done is done, right?"

Rook folded her hand into his. "You're gonna have to forgive me if I'm hard to shake after all this." He considered her fingers as if each was a unique source of fascination. "I knew if you ever came back into my life, I wouldn't be up for letting you go again."

"That doesn't sound so bad to me." Viva scooted round to face him more fully.

His expression was a sober one. "I haven't evolved all that much, V. I'm still that guy you had to walk away from."

"I was really in love with that guy, you know?" She straddled him on the bed.

"Really?" Rook fought to suppress a smile. "He was pretty overbearing, kind of a know-it-all."

"Mmm…yeah…yeah, he could be those things. But his body is amazing and he's quite stunning in bed."

Rook had to laugh then. "We can't spend all our time in bed, though, remember?"

She shrugged. "Well, it's not a deal breaker and like I said...I love you, remember?"

"I remember." He'd been spanning the lush length of her thighs with his palms. They traveled up to curve about her waist and he tugged to set her nice and neat against a renewed erection.

Viva wanted to melt, even as her heart sank in reaction to the fact that he'd yet to reciprocate her emotional confession. Still, happiness continued to mount and she forgot her disappointment when he nudged her close for a kiss.

"I love you," he said softly, simply against her mouth.

Her sinking heart was suddenly in her throat and the resulting kiss was more than a greedy claiming. It was a confirmation that their hearts were again as one.

Words of promise and love renewed were whispered deep into the earliest hours of the morning. This, followed by more lovemaking, interrupted by lengthy bouts of sleep, followed by more lovemaking.

Rook didn't make a move to head into work that morning and Viva wasn't about to call his attention to the fact. Sunlight was reflecting blindingly bright off the snow-capped landscape around ten that morning when they decided it might finally be worth checking out another area of the house besides the bedroom.

While Rook went to the kitchen to begin breakfast, Viva returned to the den and set the coffee table. The plan was to eat there with the splendid mountain scenery before their eyes. With the table set, Viva returned to the kitchen to watch Rook put his culinary skills to the test. Watching the man cook was only an added benefit. Viva was more interested in watching him cook wearing only the nylon basketball shorts he'd tugged on before leaving bed. She grabbed her cell as she passed the lamp table where she'd left it last night. By the time she got to the kitchen, she was frowning into her phone.

"Trouble?" Rook had spied the look she wore when she took a seat at the other end of the wide wood-grained cooking island.

"Not sure…there're about ten missed calls from Stanton Giles. He's Bryce's agent."

The news had Rook's hand hovering over the bowl of eggs waiting to be cracked. Viva pulled a trembling hand through her hair and gave the phone a foreboding look.

"I can't take much more of this," she said. "If Stan tells me something's happened to—"

"Hey, hey, stop." Rook turned to wave off her predictions. "Find out what the man wants before you take your trip off the deep end, okay?" His stern expression softened when he saw her decisive nod.

"You're right." Viva continued to nod while she eased off the island's bar seat. She disregarded the time; the man had left ten calls, after all.

Rook forgot his breakfast duties, his focus instead on Viva across the big kitchen. Slowly, approvingly, his gaze roamed her legs bared beneath the hem of an extralarge midnight-blue sweatshirt. All she wore beneath were a pair of pink bikini briefs and the knowledge of that pleased him to no end.

Viva was greeting Stan Giles a few moments later. Rook half listened. His attention gradually returned to his cooking task as he took in the obligatory opening chatter and the series of "mmm-hmms," "okays" and "rights" Viva uttered for her part of the conversation. Her sudden gasp and hushed "what?" followed by "Are you serious?" had Rook pausing once again over the food.

When she screamed, his first instinct was to go to her. Then he saw the scream followed by five seconds of excited jumping and a hand covering her mouth to muffle more screams. He understood. The news was good. He focused on whipping the eggs into a creamy yellow froth.

"Oh?...Yeah...No, yeah, yeah, I get it. I, um, how'd he—how'd he sound, Stan?...Right...Right, no, I—I get it...Yeah, yeah I *am* excited." She turned, met Rook's gaze and smiled brighter. "Right," she said into the phone. "Yeah, okay, Stan, thanks...Okay, sounds good...All right...All right. Talk to you soon...Bye."

"Good news?" Rook was adding chopped scallions to a bowl of chopped green peppers and spinach.

"The show..." Viva began as if dazed. "Sounds like we're popular enough for a movie."

Laughter was brightening Rook's remarkable face even before the sound tumbled full and rich from his throat. The explosion of good cheer was followed by words to that effect and he came around the cooking island to grab Viva into a bear hug that took her off her feet.

"It's pretty cool, huh?" Viva's words were practically swallowed up by her laughter.

"Probably old hat for someone who's no stranger to the big screen," Rook said as he set her to her feet.

"Are you kidding?" Viva shuffled back to the island and set the phone on the counter. "The show was my first real leading role. To know it's become so popular with the audience and that the audience is big enough to get the attention of a well-respected studio…it's like a dream that keeps on morphing into something more amazing."

"Okay." Rook nodded, tilted his head as if measuring her expression. "So why do you seem sort of down about it?"

Viva let her smile carry only a few seconds longer before letting it slip. She didn't know why it still surprised her how well he knew her.

"Stan reached out to me because Murray asked him to. Stan is Bryce's agent, not mine."

"So?" Rook went back to his place at the stove.

"So why give a damn whether I hear about this or not if he plans to kill me? He asked Stan to take me on as a client. Why do that?"

"To put you at ease, maybe?" Rook gave the eggs a few more seconds of unnecessary beating. "To have you focused on good fortune instead of the threat at your back? Do you really not get that, V?" He pushed the eggs aside.

"I just don't…"

"Don't what, V? Believe he'd ever do anything so foul? I get it."

"Rook, I—I don't want to fight."

"Neither do I." He took up the egg bowl again. "I'll call you when breakfast is ready."

Viva used another minute to study him. The rigid set of his shoulders was more than a little noticeable. She agreed it was best to wait out the breakfast prep elsewhere. Before she cleared the kitchen's entryway, she heard his voice.

"He enjoyed it," Rook spoke over his shoulder, sorrow clinging to every word. "Murray. He told me to my face. I think he made a special trip back just to do it. He enjoyed telling me about you and Vossler. Grinned like an idiot the whole time he was giving me the details. He knew I was too out of it to beat the hell out of him like I otherwise would've done. He finished up by telling me that his only regret was that he couldn't tell me how much you enjoyed yourself. He must've had a conversation with Vossler about it. According to the man himself, you were very eager to please."

Viva was glad Rook kept his back turned. Her face was shining with tears that blurred her vision as they streamed her cheeks. She left the kitchen soundlessly.

Rook remained motionless until the mutinous anger engulfing him had backed off.

Breakfast was a quiet affair. Rook and Viva managed to enjoy it in the same room, though Viva wondered if that was because they ate in the den and not in a more formal setting at an actual dining table. Aside from requests to pass the fruit bowl or nods for coffee to be topped off, there was no real conversation.

They parted ways soon after the meal. Rook handled the dishes. Viva had said something about getting dressed and then reviewing her script again. She tried to close out the replay of the run-in with Murray that Rook had mentioned. But it was useless.

After she left home—the *way* she left home—there had been no one, no family. There was only Murray—*he'd* been her family. He'd been there for her through everything. Everything. From the early career disappointments, to giving her a shoulder to cry on when she continually mourned the end of her relationship with Rook.

"God..." she moaned, holding her head in her hands as she leaned against the window in the parlor.

Murray had done it. Rook was telling the truth about what he'd been told. Even all the rest, the curious accidents that had befallen others over the last several weeks... He was most likely responsible for them, as well. Most likely? Most definitely. She knew that and she just couldn't bring herself to admit it.

Knocking caught her attention. Quickly, she blinked water from her eyes and turned on the padded window seat where she'd been pretending to review the script for the past few hours. The routine had not changed much over the last day and a half. She and Rook had spent much of that time moving around each other in quiet caution. She guessed they were both afraid of saying more of the wrong thing.

Rook leaned on the doorway, his expression soft. It was the hint of playfulness she saw in his amber eyes that had her dark ones narrowing from curiosity and relief that the tension between them might be easing.

"It just occurred to me that I haven't spent this much time in the house since I brought you here." He inhaled and gave the room a speculative appraisal. "Had no idea how quiet it gets around here."

Viva smiled and waved the script. "I'm gonna know my part and everyone else's by the time we start filming. The quiet really is great for concentration." Her smile widened at his theatrical sigh.

"It's been less than forty-eight hours and I'm about to go into noise withdrawal."

Enjoying his mood, Viva laughed. "Is that a bad thing?"

"Don't know... I've never experienced it before, but I don't think I want to take any chances."

Rook lifted a finger as if to excuse an interruption. Viva watched him take the mobile from his back jeans pocket.

"So are you hinting that we need to make some noise?" she asked once he was done reading the screen.

"I think it can be arranged." He pushed off the doorway and left the parlor.

Curiosity at its height, Viva followed and drew to a tentative stop when she found him relaxed against the wall beside the front door.

"Rook—"

"I think our noise is here." He hiked a thumb toward the door.

Steps still uncertain, Viva moved to the door, opened it a crack and stepped out to the wide entryway.

At first, she saw nothing to indicate the noise Rook had promised. Then, rising snow in the distance brought a suspicious flash to her face. Three SUVs approached.

"What'd you do?" she breathed.

"Not a thing." Rook came out to watch the SUVs roll foward. "I'm totally innocent. Ask the cops if you don't believe me."

Viva laughed when she looked to the stopped SUVs and saw the cop in question step out the back of one.

Laughter then mingled with happy tears as Viva raced from the chalet's entrance to throw herself against her sister in a stifling hug.

Chapter 13

The promised noise had been delivered on once the guests exchanged the plush warmth of the SUVs that had transported them from the airport for the plush warmth of the chalet set amid a landscape of wintry white.

On hand were Tigo and Sophia, along with Linus as well as Elias Joss and his love match, Clarissa David. Rounding out the guest list was Sophia's longtime friend and Philadelphia's DA, Paula Starker.

Viva hadn't realized how starved she was for a bit of noise until she was in the middle of hearty conversation and laughter.

"I can promise you that he had no idea." Sophia confirmed Rook's plea of innocence. "We've been planning this for weeks. Everyone's had their schedules cleared—even Paula. Rook didn't know a thing until we called before leaving for the airport."

Viva squeezed a pillow to her chest and beamed at her sister from the bed. The chalet's six bedrooms were all claimed. Rook had taken the guys out to walk the property before dinner, leaving the girls to get settled in.

"Was it our conversation?" Viva asked.

"Mmm…that's what made us up our plans." Sophia hung up the last sweater from her garment bag and then rested against the entryway of the walk-in closet she would share with her fiancé. "I didn't like the way you sounded, *but*…" Slyness crept into her gray eyes. "Was it my imagination or did you and Rook look like you'd worked things out on that end?"

"For the most part." Viva tried, failed to keep the light bright in her gaze. "Like everything else between us, it's all extraordinarily complicated."

"Care to share any details?" Sophia moved toward the bed.

Viva obliged, taking advantage of the chance to vent to her sister face-to-face. "You can save yourself the trouble of telling me that you see Rook's point," she said upon completing her explanation.

"You know, I really do get it. Your loyalty to Murray. He was there for you at a time when the rest of us couldn't be."

"Is there any more news about him?"

"Not a peep." Sophia unwound a gray cashmere scarf from her neck and let it pool on the edge of the bed once she'd taken a seat on the corner. "Guess he was serious when he told you he was putting things to bed—including himself."

"Is your case still strong without him?" Viva sat

up, folded her legs beneath her while keeping possession of the pillow.

"Having him, having him *talking*, may've given us access to who's at the head of this thing. Your identification of the Greenways strengthens the connection between Murray and my colleagues currently cooling their heels in a cell." Sophia gave an exaggerated shrug while rubbing her hands one inside the other.

"We've managed to pull a few dirty cops off the streets, but the real endgamers…chances are they'll be in the wind if we can't turn Murray. Gotta catch him first, though."

"I'm sorry, Soap."

"Don't be." Sophia gave a contented grin and reached over to squeeze Viva's ankle. "We got a lot of good work done. I only hate it's put you and Rook back in a bad spot."

"A bad spot…" Viva spoke the phrase in a whimsical manner. "That's a spot we're both familiar with."

"I'd hoped the time away would give you a chance…a real one."

"I think it has."

"But Murray's still between you?"

Viva relaxed back onto the bed, her whimsical smile merging with something more stoic. "You know what, Sophia? I've got a feeling he always will be."

"I'd never even think about the office if it meant leaving this place."

Rook raised a long, sleek brow toward Elias and then traded looks with Linus and Santigo. Coming from the workaholic construction entrepreneur, the statement was very much out of character.

"Tell me when your true self decides to make an appearance," Rook urged Eli.

There was a round of laughter then. The guys had returned from their trek about the snowy grounds, but opted for a bit of conversation. The fire pit built into the back deck served as the perfect location.

"Rook, my friend, this is Eli Joss *after* a dose of Clarissa David."

Grinning, Rook settled back on the thick cushions of the wood-framed deck chair he'd selected. "So, what's up, E? Is love to blame?"

"Not a bit." Eli gave a defiant shake of his head, then caving, shrugged. "Maybe...*partly* to blame."

"So how are things goin' here?" Linus asked Rook once waves of the serious had seeped in amid the rousing laughter that had followed Eli's admission. "I thought Viva would be looking more pissed off about being babysat."

One corner of Rook's mouth lifted in a rueful smile. "We've had some breakthroughs...and some setbacks. I told her I knew about Vossler."

There was no need for further details on that score. The guys knew of their friend's struggles following Viva's departure.

"Even after I told her about that, I still think she refuses to see Murray for what he is."

"Sophia says no one's heard a thing from him," Tigo offered.

"Maybe just as well." Rook leaned forward to rest his elbows on his knees and warm his hands near the fire. "But as long as that joker's in the wind..."

"You really think he'd kill her to shut her up?" Eli asked, disbelief in his every word.

Rook let his sigh serve as his initial response. "The angry ex-boyfriend says yes." He participated when his friends laughed.

"And what does the security expert who Italy's willing to shell out a small fortune to think?" Linus asked.

"That guy..." Rook rubbed a warmed hand across his jaw. "That guy thinks she's still in trouble too."

"But not from Murray?" Tigo asked as though he'd already mapped his friend's thoughts.

Again, Rook shook his head. "No, not from Murray, but possibly from people who want to shut him up tight as they do everyone he knows."

Dinner was a hilarious and lively event. Rook had passed off his chef's cap to Sophia and Paula who whipped up a veritable feast. Conversation ran high with compliments and a fair amount of amused surprise over the culinary talents of the DA and chief of Ds. Afterward, it was a game of pool for the guys, while the girls made their way to the cozy parlor for drinks and more talking.

"Linus?" Viva called as she saw the man about to take the corridor to the billiards room. She moved close to squeeze one of his hands into both of hers. "I just wanted to thank you for coming."

"Are you kidding?" Linus's dark eyes sparkled with playful devilment and accentuated his features. "There was nothing Eli could've said, done or *threatened* to do that would've kept me away!" He laughed along with the women and then tugged the fitted sleeve of Clarissa's casual navy jumper. "Tell Eli I said that and I'll deny every word."

Clarissa pressed a hand over her heart. "He won't hear it from me." She laughed out the promise.

"I especially wanted to thank you for everything you did for Rook...before." Viva's eyes were soft, her gaze appreciative.

Linus nodded slowly while a shadow ghosted across his dark face. His gaze moved to Paula then and the woman's intake of breath was overheard by everyone nearby. Apparently, satisfied by the reaction he got, Linus looked to Viva again.

"I know what it's like to let rage take you somewhere you never meant to go. I wasn't about to let my boy experience that if I could help it." He squeezed Viva's elbow, shifted a last quick look to Paula and then continued on his path down the hall.

The satisfying meal had not only filled their stomachs, it had spurred on the need for sleep of the deepest variety.

Viva was true to her duties as hostess once everyone had turned in for the night. She made sure everything was in its place downstairs before she headed up. The parlor was her last stop. She tossed a few pillows back to their places on the love seats and was turning for the door when she saw the shadow filling the entryway.

"It's me." Rook heard her muffled curse of surprise. "Didn't mean to scare you."

"I forgot how quiet you can be." Viva coughed to relieve her voice of its quivering.

"Habit of the job," he said.

Viva could only nod as she was unable to form words with her heart lodged as it was against her larynx. In the dark, she could see Rook move steadily closer. He took her hand, squeezing it when but an inch separated them.

"I'm sorry about what happened, after your call about the movie," he was saying. "You've got a right to your opinion of Murray."

"So do you." Her heart stuttered when she felt him squeeze her hand again.

"Think we could leave this discussion alone?"

The request opened a floodgate of relief. "I'd like that," she said.

"On your way to bed?" Rook asked once silence carried between them for scarcely a second.

Viva took the olive branch to shift the conversation. "Yes, I'm beat," she sighed.

"Where're you sleeping?"

"Wherever you are." The response rushed out before she could stop it.

Rook felt the grin spread across his face when her muffled curse followed the unintended reply. "That's too bad." Playful regret hugged his words.

Again, Viva cursed herself for speaking her mind. In no mood for further humiliation, she tugged her hand free of his and moved to inch by him.

"That's too bad," he repeated, curbing the rest of his statement until he saw her steps slow and halt. "Because I'm not really sleepy right now."

Viva turned then, tilting her head and trying to gauge his expression in the dark. "I, um… I'd hate to leave you up by yourself."

"I'd hate it if you did that too."

"Guess we should go on up?" Slowly, she shaved off the distance she had put between them.

"No need to go up."

Viva's heart was then swan-diving to her stomach when she felt herself being hoisted up. The night was especially black. Even with the open floor plan and tall windows filling the space, the area remained in shadow that evening. Something about that played at the edges of her arousal. The feeling wasn't unnerving. It was electric.

The simple lounge dress she'd worn that evening was soon pooled around her feet in waves of violet cotton. Rook's every move was as enticing as it was unexpected. No chair or sofa in the parlor could comfortably accommodate his height, so he took them to the floor.

Her heart was promising to beat out of her chest as anticipation had its way with her. It was a dual assault, what with Rook plying every inch of skin he uncovered with lazy, openmouthed kisses. Just when she thought she'd predicted the path of his moves, he'd switch gears on her.

The rug offered more than enough cushion for her back and was a soothing pallet for her bare skin once he'd stripped her of every stitch. The lazy kisses resumed their travels, adoring the firm, plump breasts he cupped while his nose skimmed the satiny tops and sides.

Viva sucked in a breath when his tongue encircled a nipple that he drew into a hard suckle. The move sent her hips bucking against the pressure of a ruthless need. Her hands moved up to his and she whimpered over the heat blooming where his thumb teased the nipple he'd yet to take into his mouth.

Her whimpers gained volume when he moved on,

his sculpted mouth brushing her rib cage. He made a brief, but memorable stop to tongue her belly button and Viva couldn't smother the tiny cry that escaped into the air. Her breath hitched when his big hands slipped under her thighs and up to cradle her bottom in his palms.

Aching, Viva offered herself before she even felt him claim her, which he did with a plundering, exploring kiss that pulled a sound that was half cry, half moan from her throat. Tremors and goose bumps riddled her body in unison. His breath was lilting across her skin when he shushed her resulting outbursts. It was useless on Rook's part, especially when he began to feast on the heart of her.

Being quiet was out of the question. Viva tried, but it was pointless to try when his tongue was capable of such incredible things. Her next uninhibited cry had Rook blindly searching for one of the throw pillows she'd moved during her earlier tidy-up session in the room.

He grabbed the small accent pillow and used it to drop a few playful slaps to the side of Viva's head. Laughter mixed with her pleasure-induced sobs then. Still, she complied with his request and turned her approving cries into the pillow instead of letting them fill the guest-packed house.

Rook's feasting showed no signs of curbing. He was truly hungry for her and knew the insatiable craving wouldn't be soothed until he'd claimed her with a more potent part of his anatomy.

Viva could hear the faint crinkle of packaging and, still breathless from his handling, moved the pillow aside. She inched up on her elbows to see that he held a condom, one of several that had fallen from the jeans he'd doffed, while she was still writhing with the memory of his enthusiastic kiss. She pushed up until she was sitting and reached out to offer her assistance with their protection.

The sweetness in the gesture was more than Rook could stand. With lust and love taking over, he took possession of Viva's hips and all but yanked her to straddle his lap. He kissed her with a hunger that had her gasping when he finally let her gulp in air.

He took her in one swift stroke, bringing her down over the wide length of his erection. Viva had the foresight to know her cries would wake the house. She'd already turned her face into his neck, using the area to absorb the volume of the screams that flooded forth when he filled her.

They were entwined with each other, curled in a lover's embrace that sent low moans and hushed cries into the darkened room. Time lost all relevance as the giving and receiving of pleasure took precedence.

"I really think we should go on up now," Viva was saying later as she and Rook lay in a tangle of limbs and clothes. She joined in when he began to laugh.

"It'd be pretty inhospitable for our guests to find us sprawled out naked in the parlor," she managed to say once she'd recovered from the bout of amusement.

There was more laughter in the dark and then Rook was rolling over. Viva couldn't see him very well, but she felt his touch strongly enough. His fingertips glided across her brow and seemed more perfectly amplified in light of the fact.

"Our guests." His mouth followed the trail of his fingers across her skin. "I like the sound of that."

"You do?" Viva could barely form the words as elation squeezed her heart.

"Very much." He rested his forehead to hers, sighed. "V, about Murray—"

"Wait." She caught his hand and brought his fingers to her mouth. "Didn't we say we'd forget that and just accept each other's opinion?"

"What if I told you I thought your opinion was more right than I let on?"

"You—you do?" She cleared her throat at the repeat of her earlier words.

Rook felt the grin spread over his face. "I think maybe you had the chance to know Murray better than I ever did. I've been in this business of mine long enough to know there's always another side to the situation. Not to say the other side is right—only that it bears looking into."

"That sounds pretty mature… Do you think we're finally growing up?"

Her question sounded small in the dark. Rook's smile renewed and he leaned down to brush his mouth to her temple.

"Feels like it," he told her, his mouth then gliding down to travel over her small uptilted nose and over her cheekbones to the curve of her jaw.

Then his lips were melding with hers and they were engaged in a delicate, seeking kiss that harbored a sweltering undercurrent of desire. Tangled limbs moved into new positions as the kiss intensified. The lovers were unconscious of the articles of clothing that became more entwined between their bodies.

During the kiss, Rook chuckled softly. "Your panties are around my ankle."

"Of course they are," she purred. "I have to find *some* way to bind you to me."

He nuzzled her neck. "You don't need them. You've always had my heart and always will."

Their kiss resumed, delicacy and desire humming more urgently then.

"Rook?"

"Mmm…" His tongue tangled lazily with hers and then took full possession of her mouth once again.

Groaning, Viva gave in to more kissing. "Rook…" she managed after more deliciously languid seconds had passed. "You're vibrating."

"Damn right I am." He mouthed another curse though when he felt the vibrations and realized it was his phone.

"Should you get it?"

Rook was more interested in exploring the valley between her breasts. "Somebody just hasn't gotten used to the time change yet. Now stop talking…"

Kissing resumed, along with the vibrations moments later. Giggles overwhelmed Viva, happiness and passion for the man she loved mounting inside her. She kissed his cheek and then spoke against it. "Maybe you should answer and tell whoever it is that people here are trying to sleep…and do other things." She bit down softly on his earlobe.

"I'd like to be doing other things besides answering the phone," Rook grumbled, but took the call when the vibrations set in once again.

Viva stretched, smiled in the dark while waiting for Rook to handle the call. When a lengthy quiet followed his initial clipped greeting to the caller, the tone in his next response piqued Viva's curiosity. She was sitting up by the time his voice crept into a more lethal octave.

"What is it?" She'd watched him in the weak moonlight and could tell when he'd pulled the phone from his ear. "Rook?"

"That was the gate."

"What's wrong?" She heard the rustle of fabric and knew he was getting into his jeans. His words had sent a dull shiver racing up her spine.

Soon, golden light pooled the room from a lamp that Rook had turned on. He continued to dress while Viva squinted to adjust to the unexpected illumination.

"Looks like we gave your friend the benefit of the doubt too soon. They've got Murray outside."

Stunned, Viva could only sit unmoving on the rug as she tried to make sense of the dizzying turn of events. When she finally snapped to, she realized Rook was gone.

Chapter 14

"Sophia...authority agrees with you." Murray Dean's attractive features were relaxed, whether from relief that he wasn't dead of frostbite or by Rook's hand, it wasn't certain.

"You may not feel so cordial later." Sophia's expression was as bland as everyone else who joined them in the room.

Rook had instructed his staff to transport Murray to the house where he'd been heading before he was spotted.

"What the hell are you doing here, Murray?"

Waves of tension surged at Viva's question. The house had awakened shortly after Rook left to meet the crew en route with Murray.

Sophia sent a nod in her sister's direction. Anything Murray said needed to be shared during an official police interview. Viva knew the nod meant that her sister was willing to forgo procedure just then.

"Did you come here to kill me, Mur?" Viva asked when there was no response to her prior question.

The query sparked a flash in Murray's observant walnut-brown eyes. "Hell no, Viva! No, never. I—"

"Never? And what about what happened to Reynolds and Bevy? And these supposed burglars that Fee Fee Spikes walked in on? All a coincidence?"

"Fee…? Reynolds and Bev? Jesus, V, how could you think I—"

"Answer her, Murray." Rook's order earned him a glare from his trespasser.

"You'd like that, wouldn't you?" Murray's sneer accompanied the accusation in his glare. "You'd love to make her second-guess me, wouldn't you?"

"It's not him who's making me do that, Murray."

Viva's admission had Murray slumping in the chair Rook had shoved him into when the guards brought him in.

"I didn't do this, V." His voice was weary.

"But you know who did," Rook countered.

Again, Murray glared at him accusingly but the look didn't hold. Instead, he nodded.

"What's going on with you, Murray?" Arms folded over the powder-blue PJ top she'd changed into, Viva moved closer to her agent. "What are you doing *here*? You had to know Rook would have mad security. You had to know you were walking into certain capture."

"I owed you an explanation." Murray's eyes were soft upon Viva, and then sobered with caution when he glanced toward the others in the room. "I had to try. Chances are I wouldn't get the opportunity…later.

I wasn't trying to kill you, Veev. I'd never do a thing like that no matter what type of screwy crap you've been told I'm into."

"Are you here to tell us you're innocent?" Cold laughter caged Rook's words.

"Far from it." Murray snorted and rubbed both hands across his shaved head. "I knew what I was doing."

"Why, Murray?"

Murray at first shrugged at Viva's quiet, confused question. "I wanted the gloss," he said at last. Simply. "I wanted it fast. Who could blame me?" he asked then to no one in particular. "Who could deny the attraction to it?" He studied his fingers resting idly along the edge of the table. "The life, the lifestyle…" He observed the table as though it showed the lifestyle he then imagined.

"The way those people live is insane—cars, boats, houses. And they have them just—just because… So much money…" He brought both hands to his temples and seemed to go ashen beneath his light honey complexion.

"They've got so much money and no clue what to do with it. I only wanted a piece—only a piece of that life. The great car, the eye-popping house…that would've been enough. I swore to myself that'd be enough, that I'd never be like the others, never take it all for granted.

"They did, you know?" Murray looked up to Viva then, punctuating the query with a knowing smile. "The cars and all that did nothing for them after a while. It lost its mystery, didn't grab them at all after a while." A sadness eased in alongside the acknowledgement.

"Because of that," he sighed, "they were looking for a new fix. For most of them, it wasn't even about making more money and that's when I knew the attraction wasn't in the things themselves, but in the ownership—the sheer will to acquire, the control, the power of it all.

"I'd made ins with folks on the force when I first came out to LA. My business was security and all, so our paths crossed from time to time." He looked to Sophia. "Unfortunately, my path crossed with some of your colleagues who weren't so loyal to what the badge stood for. Some actually sought me out when they heard I was from Philly. Wasn't long after that I was tied into a more direct pipeline and dealing with folks you probably shook hands with every day, Sophia."

Murray sighed, stretched his long legs beneath the table. "Mix in my studio contacts looking to dabble into more than property and vehicle acquisitions…and it was the start of a beautiful friendship."

"So they were laundering the money through the studios?" Sophia sounded incredulous.

"*Some* but those execs had their hands in lots of pies. There were tons of opportunities and tons of places to wash cash."

"And did that get you any closer to what you wanted?" Viva asked.

Murray seemed to be contemplating his answer. "For a while…yes, it did."

"And then?"

Murray looked to Clarissa seated next to Elias at the opposite end of the long table where everyone had gathered. "The tiniest ripple had a chain reaction no one could've guessed," he said. "Your aunt was as smart as she was lovely, Ms. David."

"She was." Clarissa confirmed the words, her smile fueled by the memory of Jazmina Beaumont.

"People with money like your aunt's usually leave their financial concerns to others. She and Mr. Cole were very tight." Murray crossed middle finger over index to insinuate Jazmina's close relationship to her then business manager Waymon Cole.

"He never caught a whiff that she was looking over his shoulder," Clarissa said. "My aunt's been on her own since she was fourteen, Murray. No one watched her back better than she did."

Murray gave a reverent nod. "Whatever bread crumbs she left for you to follow upset the status quo for damn sure."

"Upset, but didn't topple," Sophia noted. "There're still a few of your partners who we'd like to upset to the tune of a jail cell."

"I'd like to see that too, Chief." Murray smirked, having noticed the looks of subtle surprise that appeared on the faces of his audience. "My...*partners* are making it personal by attacking my clients."

"Threatening to kill us if we talk about anything we may have seen?" Viva asked.

"No, sweetness." Murray's smile was apologetic. "Threatening to take out all of my clients if *I* don't talk. If I don't talk and spin the story they deem acceptable, they'll keep going after my clients."

Viva blinked, her back stiffening. "They want you to confess to it all."

Murray chuckled. "As if anyone would believe the

buck stopped with me on a take that substantial. Hell, if that was the case, I'd have a whole fleet of associates handling you guys while I chill on a beach." He shook his head, winced. "Anyway, that's how they wanted it. I've been ducking and dodging, trying to stay under the radar until I could find a time and place to get Sophia's ear." He looked at the chief of detectives then. "I knew I couldn't just talk to you in Philly, so I kept an eye on your movements hoping for a chance."

"You've been following her." It wasn't a question. Tigo's voice, as dark as his expression, left no doubt as to the murderous trail of his thoughts.

"Old habits, man." Murray raised his hands defensively. "Security was once my job and surveillance was a huge part of it. She was never in any danger from me, Santigo. I only wanted a chance to tell her what I was dealing with and see if she could help me."

"Help you get out of it?" Eli asked, his voice and expression as dark and menacing as Tigo's.

Murray was already shaking his head. "Help me, by accepting the story I'll give you. The one that lays all this at my feet."

"You'd do that?" Rook's expression was more curious, not quite as dark as the ones worn by his friends.

Again, Murray was responding before the query was complete. He nodded. "My clients are my dearest friends—my only friends. Some are like family." He looked to Viva. "They are family."

Viva didn't dare blink, knowing the movement would send the water pooling in her eyes streaming down to wet her face.

"You know I can't do that, Murray," Sophia said.

"These people are serious. They laced Reynolds's

drug stash to make it look like he OD'd." Murray shifted pleading eyes to Viva. "Bevy isn't supposed to be in the hospital. She's supposed to be dead." He managed a grim smile. "Guess those defensive driving classes she had to take to prep for her role on the show paid off. But she should be dead, Viva." He returned his gaze to Sophia.

"These people are serious," he insisted.

"So am I." Sophia's eyes glinted fiercely. "I want the truth, Murray."

"Dammit, aren't you listening to me?" Murray brought his fists down on the table. "Do you think they'll let Bev live once she's out of the hospital?"

Sophia wouldn't relent. "You telling me the truth is the only way we'll get these snakes off the street. You say you care about your clients. Do you care enough to give me the truth?"

Murray regarded his hands for a long time and then he was looking back to Viva. "I never meant for this to happen."

"Oh, Murray." Going to him, Viva gathered the man's trembling hands and squeezed. She smiled when he squeezed in return, bowed his head and kissed the backs of her hands. "Do you remember the time you came to drag me out of that party Reynolds threw?"

In spite of his distress, Murray gave in to a brief laugh. "Yeah, he promoted the hell out of that party. 'Wear your white to drink the white.' Rumor was he'd gotten the liquor flown in special from his cousins in West Virginia."

Viva laughed then too. "Well, it sure tasted like the real deal." She sobered some, but a soft smile remained. "Do you remember what you told me that day?"

Murray's lips thinned and he nodded. "I told you you were better than this. Rumor also had it that Reynolds's career was circling the drain. I thought I could prevent that when he came to me looking for representation. Reynolds and most of the folks he associated with were talented as hell, but they couldn't get or keep jobs because they were too busy sleeping off highs and hangovers for most of the day.

"You'd already made a lot of mistakes in a short span of time," Murray recalled. "Out of my own selfishness, I let you because I hoped it meant you were buying into your life out there." He flicked a glance toward Rook.

"Then I realized you weren't buying in. You were trying to be something—some*one*—new. I told you that who you are got you everything you'd become and that you didn't owe anyone else for that, but you. I still believe that."

Viva nodded, recalling the old lecture that had somehow penetrated the edges of her moonshine-soaked brain. "Do you remember what else you said?"

"I said this was the coward's way out."

Viva gave his hands another tight squeeze. "You do realize these bastards are playing on your fear, don't you?"

"They're powerful people, sweetness. Your career—"

"Is one *I've* made. I don't owe anyone else for that but *me*. Knowing that, I can be brave enough to handle whatever this dishes out. Can you? Can you be brave enough to live by your own words, Mur?"

His weary expression made a slow transformation into one that showed fleeting glimpses of amusement and resolve. "I didn't realize you'd paid so much attention to what I'd said that day."

"People tend to pay attention to the truth." She gave his hands another squeeze. "They'll pay attention, Murray." She looked to Sophia, standing next to Paula, and nodded before turning back to Murray. "Give them that."

A nod gradually took hold of Murray and then he inhaled hugely as if the gesture had added fortification to his resolve. Viva cupped his cheek and he moved to cover her hand with his.

"Do you forgive me, Veev?"

"There's nothing to forgive." She squeezed her eyes against stinging tears when he drew her in for a fierce hug.

Viva warmed her hands about the porcelain mug and delighted in the tea's soothing aroma while she studied the scene beyond the windows.

Eager to get a head start on his day, Murray had insisted on going on record then and there. Sophia didn't want any more liberties taken with the man's rights than there had already been. Yet Murray insisted on at least giving the chief of detectives the names that would prove vital to her case.

The reason for Murray's insistence was no mystery. He wanted the names on record in the event that he didn't make it back to Philadelphia alive. As the man had yet to lawyer up, Sophia decided to accept the information being offered and use her mobile to record the statement.

Bundled in hats and jackets, they walked the snowy acreage behind the chalet. The mountains loomed in quiet majesty. Keeping an appropriate distance were Tigo, Linus and Eli. To maintain an additional air of propriety, DA Paula Starker remained absent from the informal proceedings. She and Clarissa met in the den to program films for an afternoon of movie watching that would begin following Sophia's chat with Murray.

Viva sipped more of the calm-inducing tea and smiled when Rook walked into the kitchen. He retrieved a liter bottle of juice from the fridge and indulged in a generous gulp once he was standing next to Viva at the sink.

"Don't worry, I'm sure Murray's safe," he said as he observed the meeting from the window. "He's got three bodyguards to make sure Sophia doesn't try anything."

Viva sipped her tea, smiled. "Tell them I appreciate it. My little sister can be lethal. I've had enough fights with her to know."

Once the soft laughter had settled, Rook rested a hip along the counter and faced Viva. "I'm sorry about giving you such a hard time about this, V. About Murray."

"Rook, we've been through this." Viva set her mug on the counter. "No more apologies, remember?"

"Can I at least tell you why I gave you such a hard time about it?"

"Haven't you done that already?" She faced him fully, mimicking his leaning stance against the counter.

"Not all of it."

"What's…all of it?"

"I was afraid you wouldn't be right and I wanted you to be right." He focused on the juice bottle and launched a slow pace of the kitchen.

"I've been in love with security in one way or another for as long as I can remember. Think it was since my mom first took me to the bank and I met a real live security guard up close." He smiled on the memory. "Back then, my folks thought I was so infatuated because those guys got to carry guns, but that wasn't even close to being it. Their job was to observe, to figure who needed to be watched and who was okay.

"I was fascinated by that and I tried to get as good at figuring that out as I could." His steps around the kitchen slowed. "I did get good at it. I got damn good at it. I got so good scoping things far off, it got hard to see what was right under my nose." He sighed, buried his face in his hands and then folded his arms across the burgundy shirt he wore.

"I never saw Murray coming. When he left the company and took you with him—" he raked Viva's face and body several times beneath his bright eyes "—it felt like a rock through my stomach and then the rage came and that…that was worse because it just sat there festering like some oozing sore. Hearing about you and Vossler was the lance that sent it all spewing.

"To know I was *that* wrong about someone *that* close to me…it was a devastation that had me second-guessing everything. My career was all I had. It was the only thing that made me keep getting up once you were gone. It was a half existence most of the time with the possibility of poor judgment always hanging over my head."

He turned to take another look out the window, his

expression unreadable. "This morning I discovered I hadn't misjudged him. Yes, he let himself be blinded and swayed by dazzle, but he stuck when it counted. He recognized you were in line to destroy yourself and he helped to prevent it. If I'd been wrong about him and who he was at the core, he wouldn't have told you what he did at that party. He wouldn't have given a damn about you. It's why I gave you hell every time you defended him." He smiled her way then. "I didn't want to let myself...I don't know...hope?"

Rook studied the juice bottle as if it were helping him to test the validity of the word and then he nodded. "Yeah, I—I didn't want to let myself hope and be wrong, knowing this time a misjudgment like that could've meant your life."

Viva came up behind him, smoothed her hands between his shoulder blades. "Murray betrayed you in business *and* friendship. It's not something you're expected to get past overnight, no matter how many names he gives Soap for that recording she's making out there."

Rook turned then, gathering Viva tightly against him. "What was it you said about us growing up? Maybe you had something there."

"Told you," Viva said, going to her toes to brush a kiss to his jaw until he lifted her higher for something more substantial.

Chapter 15

The day ended quietly enough. There was talk about putting Murray in the guest cottage half a mile away from the chalet, but Sophia opted for another plan. At Rook's suggestion, she decided the loft bedroom would be a better fit. Rook had been playing with the idea of turning the area into an office. It would be better suited to Murray Dean for the remainder of his stay, which was slated to be no more than another forty-eight hours at best. Time enough for Murray's official travel companions to arrive from the States to assist in his return.

The tensions of the day had leveled out as feelings of closure started to edge in. By late afternoon into early evening, the nice vibes that had permeated everyone at the onset of their visit were back on track. That had a great deal to do with the host and hostess.

There was no denying that love was vibrating powerfully between Rook and Viva.

The two had bowed out of the movie night, and early morning found them engaged in a sensual scene on the enclosed, heated veranda outside Rook's room. Snow pelted the tinted glass. The quiet tapping created a hypnotic melody that mingled nicely with the uninhibited sounds of passion filling the space. The erotic session, playing out on an oversize armchair beneath a blanket of white fleece, showed no sighs of an immediate cooldown.

When release crested in unison, Viva all but collapsed onto Rook's stunning chest. Laughter mounted in a wave of emotion consisting of satisfaction, happiness and hope.

"I wish we could stay here forever." She sighed, feeling no unease about making the admission. The words were true ones.

"Guess we'll all be following Murray's lead after the wedding." Rook placed a kiss on the top of her head.

During the previous night's dinner, Tigo and Sophia clued everyone in to what was in store for the second leg of their trip. The couple had decided to return to the States as newlyweds. Once the bride's official business was finished, the party would hit the road once again. The destination—Mexico. A private strip of beach would be the setting for the nuptials and home to the wedding party for at least a week.

"Think Sophia will kill me if I miss the wedding?" Viva curved her body tighter into Rook's chest.

"I believe your sister would take great pleasure in the chance to kick your ass for a thing like that."

Viva sighed. "Everything's such a mess, Rook."

"Not as much of a mess as it's been."

"You're in Philadelphia and I'm still in LA. Correction—I'm still in LA and you're a new home owner in Italy. And now there's filming for the show and with all the other projects I've got going…" A haunted look cooled her warm gaze. "We were busted up by our careers before and *that* was before we even got our careers started."

"Hey?" He cupped a hand to her cheek, waited for her to look at him. "Put the blame where it belongs, okay? Not on our careers, but on us." Resting back, he tugged her closer. "Truth is, we didn't bother to work hard enough to keep it together. We could've been fry cooks and not had a better outcome."

Viva laughed, kissed the pec that bulged nearest her lips. "There's a lot to be said for the simpler ways of making a living. Do you think we can handle the distance?"

"Don't know. I know I'm ready to stop guessing and wondering it all into a watery grave." Rook tipped her chin. "You know where I am when you decide to stop doing the same."

Before she could speak, he silenced her with a kiss that sweetly wiped everything from her mind.

Rook left Viva sleeping, pleased to see her catching up on her rest. He knew the last several hours had been a brutal ordeal but one he hoped might be the beginning of a path rebuilding between them.

He'd meant what he had told her. He'd be ready when she was ready. Something told him that he might not have long to wait.

It seemed his guests had similar plans to sleep in that morning. Rook decided to head into Belluno and tend to what had gone undone as a result of the previous day's upset. He took the time to stroll the house. He'd had Viva to thank for making it a home. She'd taken a construction of stone, brick and wood, and had given it life, warmth and the potential to be spectacular. She'd done it for him.

The view from the living room stopped him as it always did when the mountains, in all their snowy scope, stunned him with their majesty.

Though he'd claimed little more than a half hour earlier that he was done guessing and wondering, he couldn't resist wondering how long he could go without Viva until need and pure want had him going after her. If it came down to that, he believed he might actually be forced to beg.

The idea had him grinning as he made his way from the living room to the kitchen. There he found Murray Dean.

Murray choked on the coffee he'd just sipped when he saw Rook in the curved brick entryway of the kitchen. The deep flush beneath his fair complexion betrayed the effects of the steaming coffee.

"Rook—" His voice sounded gravel laden, possibly from the hurried swallow of the hot liquid. The effects could've just as easily been a reaction to the unease Rook Lourdess could instill without saying a word.

"Sorry," Murray said, his tone then a humble one as he regarded the larger man.

Rook was waving off the apology. "You're entitled to food and water—or coffee," he said as he gestured toward the mug Murray cradled between his hands.

A small, relieved breath slipped past Murray's nostrils, but he didn't appear completely at ease. "Chief of Ds gave me the go-ahead" he saw fit to share.

Smiling faintly, Rook poured himself a mug of the aromatic blend. "Wonder if the chief had to square it with her big sister first?"

Rook's demeanor must have relaxed Murray for he grinned. "I think that's who told her to tell me it was okay." Murray indulged in a little more laughter, but soon the gesture was waning as concern took hold.

"Do you think she'll forgive me, Rook?"

"I could've sworn I heard her say she did yesterday." Rook toasted with his mug and then took a sip.

"Yeah." Murray merely studied the contents remaining in his mug then. "I, um… I wasn't talking about that exactly. By now, I'm guessing you told her you know about Vossler and that I was the one who told you."

"You're sure of that?" Rook gave off a sense of maddening calm while observing Murray over the rim of his mug.

"She'd planned to tell you." Murray nodded once when he saw surprise register on Rook's face. "It was all she could talk about and that was long before she ever went to see her family back home."

"All she could talk about…" Rook set his mug to the counter.

"What happened with Vossler…" Murray worked the bridge of his nose between his fingers. "That drama took its toll on her. He didn't hurt her." Murray had looked up in time to glimpse the ferocity in Rook's eyes. "It was how she regretted it." He took a slow turn around the kitchen, the ripped cuffs of his jeans dragging on the glossy floor as he moved.

"She regretted doing it, but *why* she did it... I think that's what really—I don't know—what really wounded something inside her. And I—hell." He began to rub his hands over his head. "I felt like scum for ever putting that mess in her head about Vossler being a top guy. All so I could climb the success ladder quicker."

Rook could feel his palm tingling with a need to draw a fist. He smiled when the tingle and the accompanying upset passed. Moving to the sink, he dashed out what remained of his coffee.

"You didn't force her to do it. She knows that, so do you." *Progress.* Rook said the word silently, triumphantly.

"No, I didn't force her, but I sure as hell didn't try to change her mind about the prick either." Murray came over to toss out his coffee, as well.

Rook sent his former colleague a sideways glance. "You know we could stand here all day going back and forth over who's more at fault, right?"

Murray nodded, grinned. "You're right." Through the window above the sink he studied the almost blinding beauty of the sun reflecting against the sea of snow that served as Rook's backyard. "I'd never ask your forgiveness for this mess, Rook, but I am sorry." His tone was cautious, measuring as he spoke. "I'm sorry and that's not me going back and forth over who's more at fault here. That's me owning it."

Murray squeezed his eyes against the brilliant outdoor view as though it had in fact blinded him. He turned, leaning on the counter while massaging his hands over his head as if to clear it.

"Feeding you all that crap," he began, "it was a punk's move. It wasn't even about you. Not—not completely." Murray's shrug betrayed a helplessness.

Rook moved from the sink. He didn't begrudge the tingle he felt in his palm that time and accepted that, for him, certain triggers would never be totally silenced.

"You and Viva…the way you guys live, hell, the way you both grew up…" Murray's eyes gleamed in acknowledgement of something unseen. "Hell, man, I've wanted that kind of life forever and a day."

Rook frowned, the reaction more about confusion than temper. "What kind of life are you talking about?"

"To be rich." Murray's tone was matter-of-fact. "The kind of rich that makes people take notice when they hear your last name. The way they do with your dad and Viva's."

"Murray, it's natural to want that kind of success. *I* want it, but when you sell your soul to get it…that's when you've got trouble, that's when you know you should be backing off."

"Easy for you to say." Murray failed at producing the grin he strived for. "For people who live the life and always have, there's no mystery, no allure—"

"No attraction?" Rook recalled what the man had said the night before.

Murray nodded then in spite of himself. "Would've been great if I'd realized that before I went and made such an ass of myself."

"Sounds like we're all growing up." Rook felt the smile at his mouth when Viva's words came back to him.

"I pray I'll have the chance to find out if that's true." Murray shed the effects of his musings and turned. "I just wanted you to know I regret my part in what happened. The one thing I pray will come out of all this is for you and V to find your way back to each other."

Murray extended a hand and waited on Rook to decide whether he would take it. The decision didn't take long and soon the men were equal participants in an enthusiastic shake.

Costa Alegre, Mexico
One week later

After having endured another week of snowy seclusion, Viva was more than ready for a little sun and fun. The fact that there was a wedding to go along with it all made the journey that much more unforgettable.

The group had taken the first few days to marvel at the turquoise waters of the Bay of Tenacatita. Costa Alegre boasted miles of unpopulated beach, perfect for supreme meditation. The intimate guest list resided in an exclusive resort that Viva's connections had secured for the affair. The last-minute change in plans hadn't been a bother for Viva. As maid of honor, she'd felt it was the least she could do.

As the bride and groom had no interest in waiting to speak the vows they had planned to utter long ago, upping their wedding date had been a joy. None of the guests had had an issue with the change. Cozy three-room cottages dotted the seaside resort and were well-stocked for the visit. The setting was as quaint as it was exotic.

Viva toyed with the idea of lingering a few more days once the wedding was over and the newlyweds set off on their honeymoon.

"Think it's too soon for me to tell my clients I need a vacation?"

Rook's question prompted laughter that Viva couldn't resist giving in to. "I see our thoughts are on the same track."

"Really?" He settled down next to where Viva sat near the fire pit nestled in the midst of low-sitting beach chairs. The sun was setting and, with the chilly breeze blowing in off the water, the fire was a welcome treat.

"I've been trying to talk myself out of it."

Viva gave a curious frown. "Out of taking time off? Why?"

"Wouldn't be any fun without you around."

"Aw…" She took his admission for a tease. "Well, I'm sure you wouldn't be alone for long."

Viva's outlook was most likely accurate. The resort hostess and the rest of her female staff had given Rook, Eli, Tigo and Linus an appraising once-over upon their arrival.

"It wouldn't be the same," he was saying, stretching out his long legs and moving his sandaled feet closer to the fire. "Damn sure wouldn't be the way I'd want it. I love you too damn much, V."

"I love you." She reciprocated the proclamation on a gasp, emotion swelling when he slipped an arm about her waist and scooped her from the low chair.

Once Viva was straddling his lap, Rook simply

waited until her eyes were locked with his. "I love you too." Conviction hugged the words. "I never stopped. I never want to lose you again. I never intend to."

A sob spilled out along with Viva's watery laugh. Then she was cupping Rook's face and kissing him with everything she had.

"Now that we've traveled halfway around the world and back again, I'd say we've paid our dues." For a moment, Rook let his gaze linger on the remarkable sky of iridescent colors.

Turning in his loose embrace, Viva rested back against the man she loved and drank in the view, as well. "I'd have to agree. Do you think we could skip all the other boring stuff we're supposed to do while we work it all out and just get right to the all-is-well stage?"

"Mmm…" Rook faked a wince. "That might be tough for me. I was kinda looking forward to all the make-up sex we're supposed to have."

Viva laughed, fearing she would be unable to quell the desire to do so, she was so extraordinarily happy. "I was definitely *not* talking about the make-up sex. Do you think we could get right to *that* and skip all those long boring talks we're probably supposed to have?"

"Hmm…" Again, Rook winced. "There was actually one conversation I was looking forward to."

Confused then, Viva waited.

"Actually, it was more of a sentence."

Carefully, she turned in his lap, abandoning the sky view to study his amazing eyes. "I guess I could handle a sentence. That's not so—"

"Marry me."

Her eyes widened in tandem with her gasp. "You, uh, you know that's actually a phrase? A, um, a question phrase…"

"So it is." He bundled her closer, his expression all serious. "Do you have an answer for me?"

"Will a 'yes' do?" Her response was immediate and she adored the way it caused him to blink in surprise and then glee.

Rook nodded slowly, smiled softly. "Yeah, um…" He cleared his throat in hopes of moving the emotional lump lodged there. "'Yes' will do just fine."

He crushed her mouth with his in a kiss that had Viva humming all the way to her toes.

"So can we get to the make-up sex now?" she asked, once he'd let her up for air.

"We can get to the make-up sex now." Rook was already moving to stand with Viva in his arms where cords of muscle flexed in caramel brilliance against the late sun.

Laughter flowed as the lovers disappeared into their tiny reserved cottage. There, love was made and, at long last, a future was planned. A future together.

* * * * *

Love creates its own rules

Bridget Anderson

WHEN I
FALL IN
Love

Ascending the corporate ladder has consumed most of Tayler Carter's adult life. Now the savvy VP is ready for a well-deserved retreat. A B and B in rural Kentucky is the perfect change of pace. But her host is no unsophisticated farm boy. Rugged hunk Rollin Coleman is educating Tayler in the wonders of natural food and down-home passion. Can he count on Tayler to leave her fast-paced world behind and together create a place they can both call home?

COLEMAN HOUSE

"Humor, excitement, great secondary characters, a mystery worked throughout the story and a great villain all make Anderson's latest an especially strong book."
—*RT Book Reviews* on *HOTEL PARADISE*

Available May 2016!

www.Harlequin.com

KPBA4490516

Reunion in paradise

Grace Octavia

Under the Bali Moon

Ambitious attorney Zena Shaw loves her younger sister too much to watch her rush into a marriage she'll later regret. So she plans to prevent the nuptials in exotic Bali. But Zena's mission hits an obstacle in the form of gorgeous Adan Peters, who now regrets once breaking Zena's heart. From stunning beaches to magnificent temples, he'll show her everything this lush island has to offer—and hope these magical nights are only the beginning of forever...

Available May 2016!

HARLEQUIN®
www.Harlequin.com

KPGO4500516

The Barrington
Brothers. New York's
most irresistible
bachelors.

NICKI NIGHT

HIS
Love
LESSON

Chey Rodgers is ready to live life on her own terms. Completing
her undergrad degree is step one—but getting snowed in with a
sensual stranger isn't part of the plan! Chey never expects to see him
again, until her new professor walks into the classroom! Successful
attorney Hunter Barrington has one semester to prove himself at his
alma mater. A secret romance with his student could cost him his
academic future. Will Hunter and Chey be able to avoid scandal and
attain their dreams without sacrificing their passion?

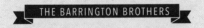

THE BARRINGTON BROTHERS

Available May 2016!

www.Harlequin.com

KPNN4520516

REQUEST YOUR FREE BOOKS!

2 FREE NOVELS
PLUS 2 FREE GIFTS!

KIMANI™ ROMANCE

Love's ultimate destination!

YES! Please send me 2 FREE Harlequin® Kimani™ Romance novels and my 2 FREE gifts (gifts are worth about $10). After receiving them, if I don't wish to receive any more books, I can return the shipping statement marked "cancel." If I don't cancel, I will receive 4 brand-new novels every month and be billed just $5.44 per book in the U.S. or $5.99 per book in Canada. That's a savings of at least 16% off the cover price. It's quite a bargain! Shipping and handling is just 50¢ per book in the U.S. and 75¢ per book in Canada.* I understand that accepting the 2 free books and gifts places me under no obligation to buy anything. I can always return a shipment and cancel at any time. Even if I never buy another book, the two free books and gifts are mine to keep forever.

168/368 XDN GH4P

Name _____

(PLEASE PRINT)

Address _____ Apt. #

City _____ State/Prov. _____ Zip/Postal Code

Signature (if under 18, a parent or guardian must sign)

Mail to the **Reader Service:**

IN U.S.A.: P.O. Box 1867, Buffalo, NY 14240-1867
IN CANADA: P.O. Box 609, Fort Erie, Ontario L2A 5X3

Want to try two free books from another line?
Call 1-800-873-8635 or visit www.ReaderService.com.

* Terms and prices subject to change without notice. Prices do not include applicable taxes. Sales tax applicable in N.Y. Canadian residents will be charged applicable taxes. Offer not valid in Quebec. This offer is limited to one order per household. Not valid for current subscribers to Harlequin® Kimani™ Romance books. All orders subject to credit approval. Credit or debit balances in a customer's account(s) may be offset by any other outstanding balance owed by or to the customer. Please allow 4 to 6 weeks for delivery. Offer available while quantities last.

Your Privacy—The Reader Service is committed to protecting your privacy. Our Privacy Policy is available online at www.ReaderService.com or upon request from the Reader Service.

We make a portion of our mailing list available to reputable third parties that offer products we believe may interest you. If you prefer that we not exchange your name with third parties, or if you wish to clarify or modify your communication preferences, please visit us at www.ReaderService.com/consumerschoice or write to us at Reader Service Preference Service, P.O. Box 9062, Buffalo, NY 14240-9062. Include your complete name and address.

KROM15

Turn your love of reading into
rewards you'll love with

Harlequin My Rewards

**Join for FREE today at
www.HarlequinMyRewards.com**

Earn **FREE BOOKS** of your choice.

Experience **EXCLUSIVE OFFERS** and contests.

Enjoy **BOOK RECOMMENDATIONS**
selected just for you.

PLUS! Sign up now
and get **500** points
right away!

Earn
**FREE
REWARDS**
HarlequinMyRewards.com
Join
Today!

MYR16R

THE WORLD IS BETTER
WITH
Romance

Harlequin has everything from contemporary, passionate and heartwarming to suspenseful and inspirational stories.

Whatever your mood,
we have a romance just for you!

Connect with us to find your next great read, special offers and more.

f /HarlequinBooks

🐦 @HarlequinBooks

www.HarlequinBlog.com

www.Harlequin.com/Newsletters

⬥ HARLEQUIN®

A *Romance* FOR EVERY MOOD™

www.Harlequin.com

SERIESHALOAD2015

SPECIAL EXCERPT FROM

H HARLEQUIN®

Mariah Drayson is set to run the Seattle branch of her family's legendary patisserie. And when she and high-end coffee importer Everett Myers join forces, he knows they're a winning team. But is Mariah prepared to reveal the secret that could cost her a future with Everett?

Read on for a sneak peek at
CAPPUCCINO KISSES, the first exciting installment of
Harlequin Kimani Romance's continuity,
THE DRAYSONS: SPRINKLED WITH LOVE!

"Everett." She swallowed the lump that suddenly formed by having the businessman yet again in her crosshairs.

"Hey." He smiled, showing off his sparkling white teeth.

"Hi." Mariah didn't know why she couldn't think of anything but a one-syllable word, and her heart was hammering in her chest.

"Surprised to see me?"

"Actually, no, I'm not," she replied, finding her voice. "You've been persistent, so I doubted today would be any different."

"Is that why you dressed up for me today?" Everett asked, raking every inch of her figure with his magnetic gaze.

Mariah started to say no, but knew it would be a bold-faced lie, so she led with the truth. "What if I did?"

HKMREXP0516

Everett's eyes darkened and his expression shifted from flirtatious to something different, something she didn't recognize but knew to be dangerous. "Come from behind the counter and I'll show you."

Mariah wasn't sure she wanted to leave the safety that the counter provided. Everett looked as if he was ready to pounce and she wasn't certain she could or would fight him off.

"Mariah." He said her name again and it sounded silky and seductive coming from his lips.

She instinctively obeyed, ignoring the warning signals going off in her brain to beware. When she rounded the corner of the counter, Everett captured her hand and brought her forward until she was inches from his face, from his lips. Sensuously full lips that she had a hard time not focusing on.

"I'm glad you've come around to seeing things my way," he said, as his large hands skimmed over her forearms.

"Did I have much choice?"

He chuckled. "No, I didn't plan on giving up. But I have to admit that I didn't come here solely to see you."

"No?" She tried not to appear offended by the comment.

"Don't look so crestfallen," he said, caressing her chin with the pad of his thumb. "I have a business offer for you."

Why did he have to keep touching her? It was scrambling her brain and she couldn't think straight. "B-business? What business would you and I have?"

*Don't miss CAPPUCCINO KISSES
by Yahrah St. John, available June 2016
wherever Harlequin® Kimani Romance™
books and ebooks are sold.*

Copyright © 2016 by Yahrah Yisrael

HKMREXP0516